PERLE
OF
WISDOM

PERLE
OF
WISDOM

A Once Upon Academy Story
Book 1

Perle & Zeke

MARIE LONG

Perle of Wisdom
(Once Upon Academy: Perle & Zeke, Book 1)

Published by Chikara Press

Cover design by Claire Holt (Luminescence Covers)
www.luminescencecovers.com

Printed in the United States of America

10 9 8 7 6 5 4 3 2 1

ISBN: 978-1-7364913-8-6 (paperback)
ISBN: 978-1-7364913-7-9 (eBook)

PERLE
OF
WISDOM

CHAPTER 1

Forest birdsong emanated from the black, cat-shaped white-noise device sitting on Perle's night table.

Perle groaned. Keeping her eyes shut, she rolled over in bed, facing her back to the sounds. "Hey, Sara, stop," she muttered groggily to the machine, drawing her knees to her chest in a fetal position.

The birdsong and nature sounds continued, becoming louder and more obnoxious.

Perle cringed. "*Hé, Sara, arrête!*" she repeated a little louder, this time in French.

Still not opening her eyes, she waited a moment, but when the machine continued to ignore her command, she grumbled, rolled back over, and groped around until her fingers tapped the smooth top of the speaker. A tingling sensation rushed through her fingers and up her arm, and the sound of chirping birds halted with a fizzle and a pungent burning odor.

Perle quickly withdrew her hand and bolted awake. Her black cat, Nuit, who was curled up at her feet, yowled and jumped in shocked fright. His gentle, vibrating warmth at Perle's feet disappeared.

Perle examined her hands. Tiny electric streaks coursed across her palms then disappeared. She whipped her head around to look at the white-noise machine and noticed a small stream of smoke rising from its speaker. *Nooo!* She'd damaged three white-noise devices in four months due to her uncontrollable powers. The employees at the local electronics store practically knew her by name from her repeated visits.

Perle yanked the machine off the night table and examined it. "Not again," she grumbled, giving the device a shake, hoping to rouse it back to life. After a few moments of turning knobs, flipping switches, and mashing buttons, the serene sound of chirping birds resumed, emitting from the speaker. She exhaled a deep sigh of relief. *Thank the stars.*

Nuit sat on the fur rug at her bedside and looked up at Perle with curious golden eyes. Then he let out a soft meow.

Smiling apologetically, Perle reached down to touch her pet. "It's okay, Nuit." Her fingers grazed Nuit's back. His black fur rose, then a spark of static shock stung Perle's fingertips. "Ouch!" She winced, rubbing the pain.

Nuit meowed and hissed, then bounded out of Perle's bedroom. Sunlight filtered through the sheer white curtains and touched Perle's face in a warm greeting. She basked in the peaceful moment, then her eyes traveled to the red-circled date on her wall calendar.

She gasped. *Bookmobile day!*

She hopped out of bed, threw on a yellow, flower-printed sundress she blindly grabbed from her closet, and stepped into a pair of matching flats on her way out of her bedroom. Racing toward the kitchen, she bunched her thick, coiled hair back into a bun and secured it with a hair clip. The house was still quiet. Perle figured her parents were still asleep. The two of them had a busy night last night, showing off their newest wines at the annual *Foire Aux Vins*, one of France's many esteemed wine-pairing events, which occurred in the neighboring town of Riquewihr.

In the kitchen, Perle retrieved her bagful of books to return and fill a small pouch of freshly picked blueberries from the refrigerator to tide her and Nuit over until they returned later for a proper breakfast. Nuit waited at the front door of the common room. She fed him a blueberry, plopped a few in her mouth as well, then headed out the door. She bounded down the cobblestone stairs, which were lined with flowerpots overflowing with purple irises. A small rose garden sat in the front of the cottage, adding to the colorful appeal of the home's exterior.

Perle rounded the side of the ivy-covered stone cottage and retrieved her bright-yellow cruiser bike. "Come on, Nuit," she called, placing her book bag in the front basket. The cat hopped into the basket as well and nestled in. Perle wheeled the bike toward the main road.

"Don't hog all the space." Perle chuckled. "I have four new books I want to get this week."

Nuit meowed in protest.

Perle pedaled as fast as she could, racing along the narrow stretch of road lined with grape vineyards separated by dense forest. Her heart raced as she rode faster, inhaling the pleasant scents of moonflowers and rose blossoms from the endless flower fields she soared past. Fifteen minutes later, she rode into town and headed straight for the distinctive van painted in various abstract colors. The van's convertible side panels were flipped up, revealing several shelves of different books. A large wooden pop-up sign affixed to the roof of the van read *Livres d'amour* in bright-red letters.

Thanks to her mother's book-loving encouragement when Perle was younger, she had always found her own peace and entertainment in the plethora of books she would bring home when the local bookmobile made its bimonthly stop in town.

Nuit hopped out of the basket as Perle leaned her bike against a nearby streetlamp. She grabbed her book bag and rushed toward the growing crowd of local families and children and tourists. She squeezed through the tight crowd, her heart pounding at the thought that she might be too late. The bookshelves were thinning, the closer she maneuvered toward the front. Most of her anticipated titles had been quickly swiped away. The lone librarian, a lithe, beautiful woman in a long, flowing blue dress, stood off to the side holding a tablet computer in her hands, tending to patrons who were ready to check out their books.

Perle's eyes zeroed in on the spine of one of her anticipated books, *The Stars of Envy* by one of her favorite authors, Pierre Favreau. She grinned at the prominent gold spine that sparkled in the light like magic. More books left the shelves as she slowly shuffled forward. She never took her eyes off the glittering unicorn symbol that branded all of Favreau's books. She squeezed and sidled around a small child and reached for the middle shelf.

The sparkling book was suddenly yanked away by another woman, who proceeded to the checkout station.

Perle balled her fists, anger and frustration fueling a spark of fiery warmth in her palms. *I saw it first!* She pushed her way through a wall of patrons and was about to confront the woman when she noticed a little boy holding the woman's hand. Handing the book and a library card to the attendant, the woman smiled politely.

"I've been looking forward to this book for months," the woman said. "I'm going to devour it during the train ride to Paris to visit my husband."

The attendant beamed, her creamy, snow-white face glowing with an aura of happiness. "Oh, that's wonderful. I do hope you have a lovely trip." She inclined her head, strands of long, curly, silky white hair cascading down her rosy cheeks.

Perle's frustration ebbed, the heat from her hands dissipating. The poor mother needed a good book for her travels. Perle dismissed the notion of confronting her and, instead, turned her attention to the kindly attendant, who tended to the next patron. Perle noticed the woman's name tag—affixed below a glittering rose-shaped brooch—which read "Giselle." *When did she start working at the library?* Perle wondered, realizing she hadn't seen the woman before.

Letting her thoughts simmer, Perle turned back to the bookshelves, which were virtually empty save for a few hardcover children's books. She sighed deeply, her shoulders slumping. She could try her luck venturing to the library in the next town to find the books she wanted, but she doubted she'd have much luck. Favreau's books were hot sellers, and they were on and off the library shelves in a flash. Besides, it was close to eleven o'clock in the morning, and Perle was getting hungry. Surely, her parents were awake by now.

Perle trudged to the drop-off box beside the bookmobile and gingerly emptied her bag of borrowed books.

"It's too nice of a day to have a long face," Giselle said softly.

Perle blinked out of her thoughts and realized the crowd was starting to leave.

Giselle rose from her chair and swept over to Perle, her flowing dress moving like a sparkling waterfall. The seemingly ageless woman was tall, thin, and walked gracefully with a ballerina's gait. "Are you all right, miss?" she asked.

Perle rubbed the back of her head. "I'm all right, just disappointed that I didn't get here fast enough to grab the books I wanted."

Giselle smiled reassuringly. "*Oui*, unfortunately, that happens."

Perle sighed. She glanced down at Nuit, who wove between Perle's legs, purring happily.

"Don't worry," Giselle continued. "I can reserve the books you want, no problem. I'll do my best to make sure you get them when we return in two weeks." She lifted her stylus, about to type on her tablet. "I'll need your name first."

"Perle Durand."

The woman's ice-blue eyes widened slightly. "Durand? Aha."

Perle raised her eyebrows. "You know me?"

"Oh, no. The… name sounded familiar as another patron's, that's all." The woman tapped her chin and quirked a smile. "I have the perfect book for you, Ms. Durand."

Perle's heart thumped in anticipation, hoping Giselle actually had an extra copy of *The Stars of Envy*. "Wonderful! I would love to see it!"

"Though it's unfortunate that you were unable to get the books you wanted, I think you might actually enjoy this one instead." Giselle walked around the back of the van and beckoned Perle with a small hand gesture.

Perle tilted her head, curious as to why Giselle was being so secretive all of a sudden. Her curiosity became intrigue, and she followed. Alone, they stood behind the van, away from passersby.

Giselle traced a rectangle in the air with the stylus, creating a glowing purple outline. Hovering in the air, the shape solidified into a weathered, leather-bound tome etched with strange-looking symbols and a golden rose in the middle.

Perle's disappointment immediately shattered. *She knows magic!* She stared at the floating book, awestruck. "H-how did you do that?"

Giselle plucked the book from the air and handed it to Perle with a bright smile. "Oh, just a simple little trick."

Perle took the book and ran her hands along the cover's raised lettering. She sighed. "I'll never be able to do any sort of magic like that."

"Anyone with such a lovely name as Perle *Durand* is bound to have some magic in her veins," Giselle said in a honeyed tone.

"There's no magic in these veins." Perle flicked her gaze at the book, and thought about the near-accident with her white noise machine. *Only destruction.*

"Bah." Giselle waved her hand dismissively.

"What kind of book is this?" Perle asked, scrunching her brow.

"It's a magic book." A small twinkle lit the woman's eye. "Open it. Only a very special person can do so."

Perle sank her teeth into her bottom lip as she reached for the gold clasp that kept the book shut. She unhinged it with a click and slowly opened the book. As she flipped through endless pages of what appeared to be unintelligible gibberish, a strange feeling came over her. She had a sudden inclination to thoroughly understand the book. She looked up at Giselle. "How do I read this?"

Giselle gave her a charming smile. "When the time is right, you'll understand how to read it. Until then, keep it close to you always. You will soon find the many answers you're seeking once you've unlocked its secrets."

Perle blinked. *What secrets?*

"Surely you'll be in a Runes class in due time at Once Upon Academy."

Perle hung her head. Over the last two years, she'd applied four times to the elite school of magic and paranormal beings but had not yet been accepted. Just two months ago, when she'd tried again, she had been met with silence. It was enough to convince her that she didn't have what it took. Perhaps her powers were too unwieldy for the school to take a chance on her.

"I'm... not qualified for that school," she finally muttered.

"Tsk." Giselle touched Perle's chin and raised it slightly to meet her glittering crystal-blue eyes. "I sense magic in you. You are more than qualified."

Perle turned her head. "I obviously don't meet their expectations. They still haven't accepted me."

"Have patience. Besides, if you were able to open that book, then you certainly have what it takes to be a student there." Leaving Perle to her thoughts, Giselle walked back around the van and began securing the remaining books and closing up the displays. After she finished, she climbed into the driver's seat. Perle stood by and looked up at her. Giselle flashed another bright smile and gave her a small wave. "Farewell, Ms. Durand."

Perle slowly raised her hand in a faint wave and watched Giselle drive off. Once the van was out of sight, Perle exhaled a deep sigh. She stared at the book again.

Maybe this book will teach me how to control my powers, then maybe the academy will accept me.

Nuit meowed then returned to Perle's parked bicycle.

Clutching the book under her arm, Perle followed her furry friend. Giselle was a beautiful mystery, and by the way she had acknowledged Perle with a certain tone of familiarity, Perle wondered if and when she would see the woman again.

CHAPTER 2

PERLE RACED HOME ON HER bike, all smiles in anticipation of settling down with her new book. She was disappointed that she wouldn't be curling up with one of her highly anticipated Pierre Favreau novels tonight, but a book about magic sounded equally intriguing.

Nuit yowled, sinking deeper into the bike's front basket, nestling himself against the thick leather-bound tome as Perle pedaled as fast as her legs could move. Returning home, Perle parked her bike in its usual spot around the side of the cottage and retrieved her new book from the basket. Holding the book in her hands, Perle felt a slight shiver traveled down her spine. The strange sensation piqued her senses, and she looked around. *Am I being watched?* No one was there, but the feeling remained. She figured it was her mind playing tricks, or the effects of her small hunger pangs.

Perle finally shook off the feeling and marched inside the cottage to the smell of toast wafting from the kitchen. She inhaled, and her stomach rumbled. A placement was set at the white wicker dinette, and a cloth-covered plate sat on the warm stove. She dropped the book off at the dinette and raised the cloth, revealing fluffy scrambled eggs and lightly browned toast.

Movement caught her attention out of the corner of her eye, and she looked through the kitchen window at two figures—her parents—out in the grape and cherry orchard. Her father, Beau, a tall and brawny man, tended to the grape vineyard while her mother, Jolie, a beautiful woman who was short and petite, traversed the cherry orchard, picking the ripened fruit and placing them in a basket. They exchanged loving smiles as they occasionally passed each other.

Perle sighed, envious that her parents had a deep, passionate love for one another, were doing what they enjoyed, and were truly living their happily ever after. Meanwhile, Perle had yet to experience true love and acceptance, only heartbreak from a past relationship that had gone sour due to her uncontrollable powers. Since then, she'd convinced herself that she wasn't yet ready to fall in love.

The touch of Nuit's furry body against her ankles, followed by a hungry meow, snapped Perle out of her thoughts. Smiling, she gave him a small rub on his head. "All right. Let's get you a proper breakfast." She procured some leftover chicken scraps from the refrigerator and served them in Nuit's small porcelain dish.

While the cat happily wolfed down his meal, Perle toted her own breakfast to the dinette and sat. She looked over to the book, her eyes drawn to the intricate cover, its odd collection of inset jewels and runes around the border, and the embossed rose symbol displayed prominently in the center. *How do I read this book?* she thought, running her fingers along the grooves in the rose petals. One of the corner jewels, a ruby-red gem, gave off a subtle glow of white light. Perle did a double take. She touched the jewel, but nothing happened. *How bizarre...* She set aside her curiosity and finished her breakfast.

Her parents came inside shortly after. Beau effortlessly toted a large basket overflowing with black cherries, and Jolie trotted in behind him. The handles of a pair of tiny shears stuck out from one of the front pockets of Jolie's waist apron. She smiled brightly. *"Bonjour, fille.* What new books did you get today?"

Perle half smiled at her parents, then her lips fell into a frown. "Unfortunately, none, but—"

"Did you oversleep?" Beau asked, setting the basket on the food-preparation counter.

Jolie's brow furrowed. "You never oversleep on bookmobile day. What happened?"

Perle sighed and shook her head. "All the books I wanted were gone by the time I got there, but the librarian gave me this." She tapped her finger on the mysterious tome.

Jolie tilted her head, examining the cover. She placed her thumb over the gold latch and tried to flip it open, but it wouldn't budge. "Hm… it's stuck."

Perle quirked an eyebrow. "Eh?"

"Let me try." Beau walked over and attempted to pull the latch apart. He grunted and strained until his face turned red. He tried lifting the book from the table, but it remained in place. "What a strange book," he said, scratching the side of his head.

Perle pulled the book back to her, picked it up, and lifted the latch with ease. Her parents stared.

"How did you—" Beau asked.

"Giselle, the librarian, said only a special person can open it," Perle explained.

"Giselle?" Jolie's brow creased, and she looked at Beau, who shook is head, seemingly unfamiliar with the name as well.

Perle shrugged. "She seemed like a kindly woman, mysterious but very polite—and beautiful." She gushed over every detail of the woman's perfection.

A small grin crept upon Beau's lips.

Frowning, Jolie looked sideways and elbowed him. "What are *you* smiling about?"

He chuckled. "Reminds me of the times back in the academy, when all these beautiful women would approach me."

"Hmph," I don't know why you're so proud about that," Jolie said flatly.

"I'm not proud of that. It was embarrassing and laughable, really. I saw through their tricks. They were all Illusionists. Beneath that vanity, they were all ugly hags."

"How did you manage to see through an Illusionist's disguise?" Perle asked, looking at her father in awe. Illusionists were masters of disguise. As far as Perle knew, only those who were most adept at magic could see through their masks.

Beau wrinkled his nose. "They couldn't hide from my beast's keen sense of smell. They reeked of rotten eggs."

Perle laughed. "How convenient."

"Anyway," Beau continued, "I only had eyes for one woman, and she apparently didn't want anything to do with me." He smiled sheepishly at Jolie.

Jolie guffawed. "You were rude, grumpy, and had your little harem of girlfriends following you like lost puppies."

"They were definitely *not* my girlfriends." He shuddered. "I'll never forget that one woman, Tilda. She claimed she was in love with me and couldn't take no for an answer."

"That was your fault, dear," Jolie said flatly.

His eyebrows shot up. "*My* fault? All I did was say 'hi' to her once because I was trying to be nice and introduce myself to the new students. How did I know she would take that to mean I was interested in her?"

Perle looked at him thoughtfully. "You never told me that story before, Papa."

"Eh, she was unimportant." He gave a dismissive wave with his hand. "She stalked me for most of my years at the academy. She was a beautiful woman but battier than a vampire, like an annoying old stain that wouldn't disappear."

"Wow, Papa. And all because you were so irresistible at the academy." Perle laughed. "That sounds like an... interesting problem to have."

"It was miserable, believe me," Beau said, shaking his head.

Jolie frowned. "Tilda was the one responsible for turning your father into that horrible beast," she explained to Perle.

Perle stopped laughing and regarded her father with a sad gaze. "Oh my…" She had heard that particular story many times but not in quite so much detail.

"The curse also removed my past memories of your mother and my time at the academy," Beau added. "But once the curse was lifted, my memories returned. Anyway, that's all done and behind us now, and Tilda is locked away in a magical prison for her terrible crimes."

"Let's just hope you don't run into any more of your old hag girlfriends, Beau," Jolie quipped, hiding her smile.

"Giselle knew about Once Upon Academy. Maybe she was a student at one time, but I doubt she was any of your old girlfriends, Papa." Perle said, giving her father a reassuring pat on his shoulder. "She didn't seem like a crazy hag to me.

And she certainly didn't smell like rotten eggs," she added with a grin.

Beau nodded. "That's good to hear."

"I think she's new to the library, though," Perle continued, recalling the woman's distinct physical features. "I hadn't seen her before. She also knows magic. She summoned this book right out of thin air like this." Perle traced a rectangle in the air with her finger.

Beau's jaw clenched. He eyed the book warily. "Sounds like illusionist magic…"

"More like conjuration," Jolie corrected. "They're the ones who can create things on a whim." She looked curiously at Perle. "Why did she give you this book?"

Perle shrugged. "I told her about my magic problems, and she seemed eager to help." She flipped the book open. "I wish I knew how to read this—" She gasped, noticing the runes were all gone and the pages were filled with legible writing. "What the…?"

Jolie and Beau sidled around behind Perle and peered over her shoulder.

Perle pointed to the open page. "The book. It's…"

"Looks like a simple botany book about roses to me." Jolie said simply.

"But I swear the pages weren't written like this before." Perle rubbed her eyes. *Is my mind playing tricks?*

Her parents exchanged worried glances.

"I'm telling you, these pages were filled with strange runes before," Perle continued.

Beau attempted to pick up the book again. This time, he successfully snatched it up without a hitch. The book shut tight on its own. Beau started with a small, throaty growl. "I don't know what sort of magic is at work here, but I've already had to endure one curse, and I'm not about to go through another," he said.

Perle reached out for the book. "But, Papa, that's the only new book I have to read."

His expression hardened. "Find another book. This one is leaving this house this instant." He marched from the kitchen and left through the front door.

Perle deflated and sank back down at the kitchen table. "I guess it's just as well. It's not like I'd ever be able to read magic runes, anyway."

Jolie placed a hand on Perle's shoulder. "You will in due time, *fille*. Your powers manifested at a very late age." She rolled her eyes. "You can thank your father for that. At least that's *all* you got from him."

Perle sighed, her gaze flicking to the table. "It's embarrassing, you know, experiencing magical puberty at nineteen. No wonder the academy won't accept me."

"Don't say that. Once Upon Academy welcomes all who possess fantastical abilities, and you are no exception."

"Then where's my acceptance letter?"

Jolie pursed her lips and didn't respond.

Perle sank farther down in her chair. "I'm too clumsy with magic. Everyone is prepared for that school but me."

"Everyone's powers manifest at different times," Jolie explained. "The school will help you control them early on."

Still, Perle had her doubts. She could barely handle a piece of electronic equipment without risking it short-circuiting. There was no way she would be able to keep her powers under control at a magical school. *The school probably sees my clumsiness with magic as too dangerous.*

Beau returned moments later, the book gone, and instead, he held two white envelopes. "Mail came," he announced, handing them to Jolie.

She skimmed them then casually set them on the counter.

Perle eyed the envelopes, hoping one of them might be hers.

"Sorry, dear. No mail for you today," Jolie said, as though reading her thoughts.

Perle frowned.

"However…" Jolie's lips curled upward into a small smile. "I do believe there was a special delivery earlier while you were out." She looked around and furrowed her brow, tapping her chin in thought. "Now, where did I put it?"

Perle straightened in her chair, regarding her mother with interest. "A special delivery?"

"Oh yeah. I almost didn't recognize the courier when he came early this morning," Beau added. He scratched the back of his head and winked discreetly at his wife.

Perle whipped her head back and forth, her gaze bouncing between her parents. "Was it for me? Where is it?"

"I saw it around here somewhere. Where could it have gone?" Jolie's smile broadened, her eyes remaining fixed on Beau. "Do you know, dear? That letter?"

Beau's smile broadened with amusement.

Letter... Perle was nearly out of her chair. Her parents knew something, and all the suspense was killing her. "*Maman, Papa,* give me the letter, please."

Jolie casually patted the front pockets of her apron and gave a small gasp of exaggerated surprise. "Ah. *Here* it is!" She pulled out a large white envelope secured with a red seal and handed it to Perle.

Perle examined the envelope a moment, running her fingers over the raised image of a pegasus stamped into the red seal, then turned the envelope over. She spotted the envelope's sender, and her heart pounded. *Once Upon Academy!*

"Oh! Marvelous! You've finally been contacted!" Jolie said.

Perle swallowed. "I…"

"Well? Open it, already," Beau urged.

Perle took a deep breath and carefully broke the seal. With shaky fingers, she pulled out a crisp sheet of parchment. The pleasant new-paper smell wafted to her nostrils as she carefully read.

Perle,

Congratulations! On behalf of the Once Upon Academy community, I am pleased to announce your admission for fall!

The academic and personal accomplishments you have already achieved within your school and community reflect what we value, respect, and expect in our students. Ambition, compassion, and a curious intellect are at the heart of the Once Upon Academy experience. You can be proud to have joined a select group of students.

For centuries, individuals have entered Once Upon Academy and have left prepared for success in the educational and magical world. Once Upon Academy's historic rate of successfully placing 90% of its students into careers as well as the commitment to making four-year graduation possible give our graduates a clear advantage over many of their peers. We believe that our personalized education allows our students to thrive both on campus and in their professional and magical lives.

Please join us during the summer to attend freshman orientation. We understand not all of our students are able to attend, so please contact Fairy Godmother to discuss a time for you to take a tour of the academy.

When you come to Once Upon Academy, you will see just what we have to offer and how our school can help you become the person you are meant to be.

Perle, we are excited to accept you into this year's student body at Once Upon Academy. Please review the enclosed checklist for the next steps needed to make Once Upon Academy part of your future. If you have already decided to join the next dynamic class of freshmen, please sign and return the enclosed form and contact Fairy Godmother for enrollment information. Upon successful enrollment, your life will change. You will be among like-minded students who will encourage you every step of the way.

Welcome to Once Upon Academy! May all your dreams come true!

Sincerely,
Fairy Godmother
Director of Admissions/Counselor

Perle stared openmouthed at the paper, which slid from her fingers and fluttered to the floor. "By the stars… it can't be! Is this real?" she said in a shaky voice.

"Oh, I'm so proud of you, *fille!*" Jolie beamed. "You'll love it there, just as your father and I did."

Perle flicked her gaze to the paper on the floor. *It's real, all right.* At last, her dream of enrolling in the most prestigious magical school around was coming to fruition. She would miss her parents and Nuit as well. She would have to find a new routine where she would soon be going. The idea of shifting old habits was frightening, but she welcomed the change. Besides, she looked forward to seeing the academy's extensive library her mother always raved about.

Jolie retrieved the signature page from the envelope. "This is what you've been waiting for, no?"

Perle took the page. Her heart pounded in anticipation. She hadn't seen her parents prouder and happier since she'd graduated high school last year. *I'm really going to go through with this? I'm really going to make this happen?* "Oui... I just..."

Jolie's excited smile waned, as if she could sense Perle's hesitation. "I knew your letter would come. The academy saw your special gift. They will help you learn how to control that gift and become the person you're destined to be."

Perle took a deep breath then laid the signature page on the kitchen table. She scanned the parchment, down to the signature line, when the paper began to give off a faint white glow. Then, in a glittering display, a white quill pen materialized out of thin air and rested on the paper. Fresh black ink had already been dabbed on the tip of the pen.

Perle let out a small gasp, her heart fluttering in anticipation. She slowly took the pen and signed her name. As soon as she finished the final stroke, the paper glowed a brighter white. It rose from the table and hovered in the air before Perle's wide eyes. The pen slipped from her fingers and floated beside the paper. The parchment rolled itself tightly, then it and the pen disappeared in a shower of blinding white sparkles.

Perle blinked in amazement. "W-where did it go?" she asked. She looked at her parents, who were seemingly unfazed by the magical display.

Beau grinned broadly, exchanging an amused glance with Jolie. "To Fairy Godmother," he said.

CHAPTER 3

PERLE RACED THROUGH THE GRAND hall, holding a piece of toast with her teeth as she wove through the chaotic throngs of students meandering about the common area and hurrying to and from their morning classes. Perle's adrenaline rush had eventually peaked after surviving her first week of fall classes. Once her mind and body had calmed down from all the excitement of settling into her new life at Once Upon Academy, reality had hit her like a brick wall. She was back in school— a *magical* school.

She couldn't believe all of it was real. It seemed like yesterday she had been whisked away in a fancy white pumpkin-shaped carriage to Once Upon Academy's fanciful campus that sat in an unidentified location. None of the other students seemed to know where the school resided, and the professors gave her vague answers when she asked. Apparently, her parents didn't know either. It was a secret that no one but the headmistress was meant to know.

Perle gripped the leather strap of her blue messenger bag slung across her body as she zipped to the end of the hall. Reaching the sliding glass door that led to the main greenhouse, Perle wolfed down the rest of her toast and peered through the glass. The herbology students were gathered around the large planter in the back, scribbling in their small notepads. Professor Jericho gestured to a mature silverstar milkweed plant while he lectured.

Perle clenched her jaw, grumbling under her breath for waking up late. Professor Jericho didn't take too kindly to tardiness, especially so early in the semester. If it hadn't been for the rousing aroma of bacon, eggs, and toast, cooked by her roommate, Anala Firestar—an amazing chef—Perle probably would have slept through lunch.

She slowly slid the glass door open and slipped inside. Mr. Jericho's gaze remained fixed on the milkweed as he pointed out the plant's intricate parts. The other students drew closer, craning their necks and taking careful notes. Perle's eyes locked on an empty space at the back of the group, and she made a silent beeline for it. She passed an adjacent planter filled with silverstar milkweed saplings. Her arm brushed a tall milkweed that drooped slightly over the edge, and dozens of monarch butterflies scattered from the disturbed plant in a swarm of orange and black.

"When harvesting, you want to be sure that the pods are narrow and—" Professor Jericho started as a butterfly fluttered past his face.

The students gasped and muttered as more butterflies swirled around them, looking for a new milkweed perch.

In the midst of the commotion, Perle slipped between two snickering students.

Professor Jericho gently waved off another butterfly and glowered in her direction. "So nice of you to finally join us, *Ms. Durand.*"

Perle slumped her shoulders and looked away, feeling the students' eyes on her. "I'm sorry..."

"Hmph!" Professor Jericho smoothed out the creases in his jacket and continued the lecture. "Now, then. Gather around the preparation table with your milkweed saplings. I will assess your progress in successfully caring for them."

Oh no! Perle gasped, watching the students move to a long wooden table in the middle of the greenhouse. A small flowerpot containing an equally small green sapling sat before each student. Due to her rush to get to class on time, Perle had completely forgotten about her own sapling, which remained on her windowsill in her dorm suite.

She stood in an empty spot between two students and gingerly watched as Professor Jericho crept around the table, peering over each student and giving them his assessment in hushed tones. It was only a matter of time before Perle would have to face the consequences of forgetting her assignment.

A student next to her checked one of the leaves of his plant. It was Ben Spriggan, the curious red-haired son of a giant slayer. He was a first-year abjuration student who tended to be a magnet for trouble around the school. He frowned at his plant.

"What's wrong?" Perle asked him, furrowing her brow.

Ben shook his head. "Aphids. They just keep coming back like there's no tomorrow. I hate them."

"Yeah, they're pretty annoying, aren't they?"

Professor Jericho cleared his throat. "Is there a problem over there, Mr. Spriggan?" He glared at Ben from across the table, then his gaze slowly swiveled to Perle.

Perle's heart pounded, and she lowered her head as she slowly sidled behind Ben in her weak attempt to hide from her embarrassment. *He's going to call me out about my missing assignment. I know it.*

Professor Jericho finally wandered over to another student farther down the table and spoke to her in hushed tones as he observed her tending to her milkweed plant.

Perle returned to her spot and exhaled, thanking the stars that she hadn't gotten called out in front of the whole class.

Ben gave her a quick, apologetic glance then nudged the student next to him, Billy Gregor, a headstrong and somewhat vain second-year evocation student. Ben pointed out a tiny yellow aphid on one of the leaves of his own plant. "Can you do a little pest control?" Ben muttered.

Billy briefly looked at the bug with interest, then he smirked at Ben. "With pleasure." He plucked the aphid off the leaf. His eyes flashed, and his fingers glowed blue. The aphid froze into a tiny shard of ice, and Billy smashed it between his fingers. His smile grew more delighted.

Perle made a face at the two, resisting the urge to roll her eyes. Billy always seemed to look for some excuse to show off the latest spell he'd learned, not like he'd ever needed to study. He was one of the few arcana students in the school who had innate powers.

"That was unnecessary, Mr. Gregor," Professor Jericho chided with a wave of his finger. "You just destroyed a delectable treat for a hungry ladybug."

Perle straightened, hearing the annoyance in the professor's voice. Her heart thumped harder again as she watched him draw closer.

Ben cleared his throat and resumed examining his plant.

"Right. Sorry, Prof," Billy grumbled.

"Fortunately, we don't have to look very far to find some." Professor Jericho held out his hand, revealing a small ladybug that happily crawled around in his palm. "Remember, everything in this greenhouse has a purpose."

Billy nodded and carefully plucked the ladybug from the professor's hand. He placed it on his milkweed sapling and watched it find and happily devour an aphid hiding under one of the leaves.

Professor Jericho continued walking, completely bypassing Perle without so much as a glance her way, and stopped at the student on her other side. She swallowed back the tightness in her throat. *He didn't even acknowledge my missing sapling. Maybe I won't be in much trouble, after all. I can only hope.*

"Now, then." Professor Jericho gestured to another long table, where a single rose lay. "Today, you're going to learn how to create a basic herbal remedy using various parts of the rose. But first, you need to learn each part of the plant and its uses. Now, pay attention."

Perle trailed the group of students then joined them around the table, where the professor dissected the rose, piece by piece, as he continued his lecture. While the students took careful notes, Perle's mind traveled back to her dorm suite, where her rose botany book still sat at the bottom of her designer suitcase. It was strange that the book had mysteriously turned up again, when she thought her father had disposed of it the day she'd received it. Maybe he'd had second thoughts or he'd found nothing wrong with the book after all and had allowed her to keep it by sticking it in her bag before she left home. Either way, she was glad to have it back, and she would make good use of it, especially in herbology class.

The students around her began to disperse, and she snapped out of her thoughts. Class was dismissed. *Did he give us an assignment?* She caught a glimpse of some of the students leaving, noticing the only thing in their hands were their potted milkweed saplings. She exhaled slightly and proceeded to head for the exit, when Professor Jericho suddenly stepped in her path. She halted and looked up at his stern gaze.

"I am so sorry for being late for class, Professor!" Perle apologized, pressing her hands together.

"You were such a bright, attentive, and dedicated student just last week. But I've been teaching here a long time and know that such excitement is only temporary. I can usually tell a student's overall level of success based on how they apply themselves after their first week, and based on what I've seen today, you will be here for a long, long time."

Perle chewed her bottom lip. "It won't happen again. I promise."

He held up his hand and shook his head dismissively. "I've no time for apologies. I take this class very seriously. The skills you will learn may one day help save a life."

"I understand…"

"No, I don't think you do. I really hate to fail students, especially so early in the semester…"

She gasped. *Failed?* She'd never failed a class in her life. "Isn't there anything I can do to make up for my mistake? What if I show you my silverstar milkweed plant? I can get it from my room right now."

He shook his head. "No."

Perle blinked. "*Quelle?* Why? I've been taking good care of it. You can see how healthy it is." *And maybe you won't fail me.*

"If you recall my lecture last week, I told you silverstar milkweed is a very delicate and precious time-sensitive plant. Your sapling needed to be transplanted into a larger pot during a precise seventy-two-hour time frame, which ended during today's class. You were thirty minutes late, missing the entire transplanting session. If the transplant does not happen during that precise window of time, then the roots begin to deteriorate permanently. Once root deterioration happens, the plant has no hope of survival. It will wither and die in less than two days."

Perle sighed and slumped her shoulders. "So, does this mean... I failed?"

"For milkweed growing? Indeed. And unfortunately, the lessons will get progressively intense as the semester goes on."

There had to be a way to fix her situation. Intense or not, she was determined not to let one day of bad luck destroy her once-in-a-lifetime opportunity. *I have to prove that I'm meant for this school, that getting my acceptance letter wasn't a mistake.* "What if I were to pass the rest of the lessons?" she asked.

Professor Jericho shook his head again, his expression turning sullen. "It would take some miracle of the stars for that to happen, Ms. Durand."

If Perle knew one thing, it was that miracles did happen. Her parents were living examples. She held her head high and smiled broadly. "I accept that challenge."

"We'll see about that. See you bright and early on Wednesday with your next assignment—or not." He cracked a smug smile then stepped aside.

Noticing the look, Perle wondered if that was his way of encouraging her to do better. She promised herself she would make up for her mistake somehow.

After leaving the greenhouse, Perle traversed the main halls, weaving through the crowds of students headed to their next classes. She still had a few hours before her evocation class started after noon, which gave her plenty of time to locate one of her herbology classmates and find out the next assignment.

She rushed across the scenic campus, following a short, winding cobblestone path through the woods and over a narrow stream. The late-morning sun touched fields of colorful tulips and daisies that flanked the path in a carpet of colors that moved with the light breeze. Once Upon Academy's campus looked like it had been taken straight from one of the many fairy-tale storybooks Perle had loved reading as a child. It seemed she was living her childhood fantasy.

She noticed the back of a man standing at the entrance to the dormitory building. As she drew closer, she noticed him playing with a small ball of purple energy. He balanced the ball on one finger then juggled it between his hands.

Perle let out a sigh of relief. She never thought she would be so happy to run into Billy again. She knew he'd probably taken careful notes about the rose assignment so he could incorporate his newfound evocation spells with it.

"Billy." She caught up with him, gently placing her hand on his shoulder.

He started then closed his hand, making the controlled ball of energy disappear in a flash. He spun around, took one look at Perle, and exhaled. "Oh, it's you."

"*Bonjour.* I could really use your help in getting the new assignment from herbology class."

His face scrunched slightly. "Why? You were there."

"I was, but... ah, I forgot to write it down. I was still taking notes from the lecture." She fumbled in her messenger bag for her mini notebook and a pen and prepared to take notes.

Billy shrugged. "Right. Well, Prof wants us to make a rosewater healing salve from an entire rose."

She scribbled. "That's all?"

He nodded. "He said every part of the plant has a purpose. I took three pages of notes about it, and I don't have time to share."

She pursed her lips then put her writing utensils away. Normally, she would be worried about how, but knowing she had an entire rose botany book in her possession eased her nerves. With the help of that book, she would easily pass Professor Jericho's assignment. "Fair enough, *merci*." She prepared to leave. "By the way, you realize it's forbidden to practice evocation spells outside the designated classes and areas around the school, right?"

He blew a raspberry. "It's only forbidden if you get caught. Besides, the rule is *harmful* spells."

"Most evocation spells are harmful in some way."

"I don't intend to harm anyone, just break up the fight that's about to go down in there." He jabbed his thumb toward the dormitory entrance.

Perle furrowed her brow then peered inside. A group of students converged under the immense crystal chandelier in the main atrium. Two young men stood in the middle, facing off with each other. They were eye to eye. The taller, slightly burly man with short brown hair was Will Cormoran, a second-year who was also on the fencing team. The brute loomed over the shorter redhead, Ben Spriggan.

"You need to stop spouting idiotic stories, Ben!" Will growled.

Ben held his hands up in surrender. "There's one in the basement right now, I swear!" Ben pleaded.

Laughter and random chatter swept among the crowd.

Will gritted his teeth and grabbed two fistfuls of Ben's shirt. "I said enough! You're embarrassing me right now. Why in the stars was I cursed with you for a roommate?"

Frowning, Perle made her way inside and sidled around the group of spectators. It was only the second week of classes, and she had seen Will and Ben publicly at each other's throats three times already. *Maybe they're brothers*, she figured, though she didn't dare ask either of them for fear of being very wrong and ending up in the middle of one of their heated arguments.

It was probably best that she didn't stick around for too long. One of the academy's faculty would surely find them and break up the commotion, and the last thing she needed was to be on any more of the faculty's negative radars.

She made her way toward the grand staircase leading up to the student suites but suddenly collided with something solid—a wall. She looked up. *No, a man...*

Her breath hitched. The tall young, clean-shaven man with silver-streaked black hair looked down at her with dark, foreboding eyes. The world around her grew smaller. *Ezekiel Wolfson*, the dormitory's resident assistant. He was only a second-year, but his tough-as-nails, no-nonsense attitude gave him a notorious reputation among the student body. Some wondered how the son of the Big Bad Wolf had been given such an important role at the academy. Perle knew better than to question the faculty's choices, or more accurately, the headmistress's.

Zeke's eyes averted to the commotion then narrowed. His rigid jaw tightened. A low, guttural growl rumbled from his throat. He shoved past Perle, and as he made his way through the circle of spectators, an ear-ringing hush fell over the atrium. Many sets of eyes widened. Jaws dropped open. Will and Ben ceased their arguing and looked toward Zeke, who stood before them with his well-defined arms folded across his broad chest.

Will released Ben's shirt and took a step back. "Uh, h-hey, Zeke. What's happening?" Will stammered.

Ben cast Zeke a fearful smile that looked more like a grimace. Ben gave him a small wave.

Zeke's head turned from Ben to Will. "You two woke me up," he said gruffly.

Will's hands began trembling. "I-I didn't mean it. Ben's telling stories again, and—"

"Enough!" Zeke barked. He pointed to the entrance. "Either take your little squabble outside, or I'll settle it *my* way." He took a deep breath and flexed, making the muscles in his chest and arms bulge and causing his overall stature to appear larger.

Chaos reigned in the atrium as Will, Ben, and the rest of the students dispersed like frightened mice. Some scrambled up the stairs while others headed for the exit. Perle ducked out of the way of the stampede of frightened students and continued watching the commotion safely behind the banister.

As the last student disappeared, silence returned to the atrium. Zeke deflated with a heavy sigh. He spun and headed for the stairs, spotted Perle, then stopped.

She felt her throat constrict as she locked eyes with Zeke for what seemed like an eternity. Beneath his brutish demeanor, she could sense a certain charm about him. He was cute, but she knew a guy like him wouldn't want anything to do with someone like her.

Zeke's eyes narrowed, then he sneered and headed upstairs. When he was out of sight, Perle slipped out from her hiding spot and exhaled slowly. Her mind refocused on getting a head start on her herbology assignment. She climbed two flights of stairs to the third floor and raced down the wainscot-lined hallway to the door of her dorm suite. She pulled a gold necklace from under her shirt, retrieving an ornate gold key. She placed the key into the Old English-style lock, and the door emitted a subtle golden glow. The lock clicked, and the door creaked open.

Entering the cozy two-bedroom suite, Perle was immediately smacked with the strong aroma of basil and onions. She followed her nose to the kitchenette, where her dragon-shifter roommate, Anala, stood cutting up onions and red peppers and throwing them into a skillet. Anala took a breath, her slit-pupil light-brown eyes emanating a fiery glow, and exhaled a small fireball onto the gas burner, igniting it. She hummed a lighthearted tune while she casually mixed the vegetables.

Perle's stomach growled despite having eaten a late breakfast. But with Anala as a first-year culinary student, Perle was spoiled almost every day with extravagant meals, many of them reminiscent of the ones her father had often cooked. "Mmm. What are you making this time?" Perle asked, approaching the stove.

Grinning, Anala stirred some tomatoes and herbs in a large saucepan. "Our assignment was to make a dish with fifteen ingredients or less that involved a tomato. I chose ratatouille because, well, you've been my muse." She winked.

Perle beamed. "*Mon papa* always makes the best ratatouille."

"Great. Then you can be my official taste tester."

"Like I have been for every other French cuisine you've made?" Perle chuckled.

Anala stirred the vegetables in the skillet. "Hey, it's your fault, being my roommate. I've practically fallen in love with French cuisine because of you, and I have the top grade in class so far. Win-win."

Perle's smile fell. *Speaking of grades…*

Anala slowed her stirring. "What's wrong?"

Perle shook her head. "I don't want to talk about it." She left the kitchenette and headed for her room.

"If it's relationship troubles, you're not alone," Anala called.

Back in her room, Perle rummaged through the few remaining items in her suitcase, which were mainly sentimental things.

"At least half the females in my class have ended or are in the process of ending relationships," Anala continued.

Half listening to her roommate, Perle pulled out photos of her parents and some of her favorite books from among the items. She reached the bottom of the suitcase, where her rose botany book sat. The embossed decorative rose on the cover gleamed like new. As she held the book in her hands, a familiar feeling came over her again, the same feeling she'd felt when Giselle first gave her the book. Her mind became clearer about her current issues, like how she was going to ensure that she passed her upcoming herbology assignment as well as find a way to miraculously restore her milkweed plant. She glanced at her windowsill where the lonely sapling sat, soaking up the early-afternoon sunlight. It looked healthier than ever, contrary to Professor Jericho's warning, but just to be safe, she quickly transplanted the sapling into a larger pot and returned it to the windowsill. She made it a point to check on it again after she paid a visit to the grand library.

"I must've totally freaked Vahn out when I showed him a new fire trick during study hall." Anala continued rambling as Perle returned to the kitchenette with the book clutched in her arms. "His face was whiter than a ghost's." Frowning, Anala slowly stirred the tomato mixture.

Perle furrowed her brow. "I thought you said he had a crush on you."

"Well, he was apparently leading me on. I think he's scared of fire. He's found some excuse to duck out of every fire-based lesson we've learned so far in Ms. Fitcher's evocation class."

"How bizarre."

"You're telling me. I mean, why would you take up evocation class when many of the lessons are fire based?" Anala added chopped eggplant and zucchini and the skillet of sautéed onions and peppers to the saucepan.

"Actually, Frost Beam was one of the first elemental spells we learned in evocation class." Perle cringed inwardly, realizing that she still hadn't perfected the spell, unlike some of her other classmates. "I think he's just scared of the fact that you're a dragon."

Anala blew a raspberry. "One of Vahn's close friends is a dragon"—she rolled her eyes—"an ice dragon, but a dragon nonetheless. I guess guys are weird no matter where you go, here or back home in Lanai."

"I'm sure he can't be any weirder than Zeke." Perle chuckled. "Seriously, is he always so… gruff? He was intense."

Anala halted her stirring and looked at Perle with wide eyes. "Wait. You ran into Zeke?"

"Literally." Perle winced then recounted her earlier encounter.

"So that's what all that noise was about earlier," Anala said. "You're lucky he was in a good enough mood to let you go. No one messes with Zeke."

"What's the deal with him anyway?"

"Well, I heard that *technically,* he should be a third-year student by now, but he's been held back for so long, I think he's pretty much given up trying to advance."

"Why did he get held back?"

Anala shrugged. "Who knows except the headmistress?"

No wonder he's so bitter. Perle frowned, wondering what his whole story was and why he was there. She would love to understand him.

"Want a taste?"

Perle looked at Anala, who held out a wooden spoon full of steaming ratatouille. As Perle was about to give in to the tempting taste, she felt a soothing warmth travel through her hands and up her arms. She could hear the sound of her own heartbeat very clearly in her ears. She started. *The book...* She was reminded of her priorities and that she needed to get to the library as soon as she could before her next class. She reluctantly shook her head. "Perhaps later. I need to do some serious studying at the library."

Anala's eyes dulled. She pulled back the spoon and tasted the portion herself. Her face suddenly lit up again. "Well, I think it tastes awesome, but I may be a little biased." She gave Perle a dismissive wave. "Go on, then. Don't study too hard."

Perle smiled slightly then raced out the door. As she headed for the stairs, she felt warmth in her hands and arms again. She examined the book closely. It emanated a faint white glow, which pulsated in the same tempo as her fast-beating heart.

CHAPTER 4

Seven massive floors of endless, book-stuffed, floor-to-ceiling shelves graced the academy's grand library. Just entering the magical place overwhelmed Perle, and she couldn't imagine her fast-reading bookworm of a mother being able to get through more than a small section in her entire lifetime. The library was far beyond anything her parents had described. It was heaven, a second home, a dream she didn't want to wake from.

It took Perle every ounce of willpower to not peruse the fiction shelves and get lost in their magical fairy tales and happily ever afters. No, she was there for one purpose, and she had less than an hour before she had to head to her next class.

She made a beeline for the botanical section and claimed a seat at one of the empty long tables in the reading area. She placed her rose botany book on the table and ran her hand across the embossed cover. She would start with that book then grab others from the shelves to supplement her studies.

As her fingers grazed the raised edges of the rose petals on the cover, she felt the warm feeling again. The sound of her steady heartbeat thrummed in her ears. Whatever magic was at work seemed far too advanced for her to comprehend. Similarly, a place like Once Upon Academy was full of all sorts of magic she had yet to understand. But she hoped that one day she would grasp that knowledge and unlock the school's many secrets.

She ran her thumb along the gold latch on the side of the book and flipped it open. A brief tingling sensation ran from her fingers all the way up her arm then disappeared. She opened the book and discovered the pages were filled with strange runes and unintelligible symbols.

She blinked. *Again?* She flipped through page after page of runes as she recalled the first time the phenomenon had happened when she'd first showed the book to her parents—but back then it had also seemed that the runes were visible to her eyes only.

A chair beside her rumbled as it slid back, and someone plopped down. Perle looked up at the lanky ginger, Ben Spriggan, who cast her a crooked smile. "Hey," Ben greeted.

His presence put her on edge. She looked around, afraid she might end up in the middle of another confrontation. "Where's Will?" she asked.

Ben snorted. "Who knows? Who cares? Probably out trying to look for a date again." He shook his head. "Kinda feel sorry for the big lug. He's such a helpless romantic."

Perle cracked a smile. "I'm sure he'll find someone. This is a school of happily ever afters, no?"

He shrugged. "Depends on who you ask. I mean, c'mon. You think someone like Zeke, son of the Big Bad Wolf, will ever find his happily ever after?"

She pursed her lips. *My father did...*

"Anyway," Ben continued when she didn't respond. "I was returning a book when I saw you sitting here alone, so I thought I'd stop by and say hi and apologize for drawing attention to you with Old Man Jericho. I didn't realize you didn't have your plant. Geez. That was crazy."

She smiled at the sincerity of his words. "It was my fault for forgetting it, but I accept your apology."

"Oh... right..." He scratched the back of his head.

The question was on the tip of her tongue, and her curiosity got the better of her. "Okay, I have to ask. What's up with you and Will?"

"Eh..." Ben waved his hand dismissively. "We've got sort of this love-hate relationship going on. I love him like a brother and a friend, but he sure knows how to get under my skin."

"What were you two arguing about earlier?"

He blew a raspberry. "He was accusing me of making up stories, said I'm the reason women don't want to date him because he's always seen as associating with the 'weird guy.' Whatever. He doesn't hear what I hear because he's always out trying to chase his next fling."

Perle's interest was piqued. "What do you hear?"

Ben's face turned slightly pale. He gave a nervous glance to his left and right then scooted his chair closer. "There's something living in the basement, or someone. It makes a weird, high-pitched cry every so often."

She arched an eyebrow. "What?" *No wonder Will thinks Ben's crazy,* she thought.

Ben looked at her, then his gaze hardened. He frowned. "You don't believe me either. Well, I know what I heard. I'm not making this up."

"I didn't say I didn't believe you," Perle said.

"You didn't have to say anything. That look on your face said everything."

Perle shrugged. "Maybe it's an illusion student playing tricks."

"Maybe. I wouldn't know. I'm studying abjuration. It's been going on since classes started last week. The sounds always happen at night, and I've barely been able to get any sleep because of it."

"I wish I knew for sure. Haven't you told anyone about it?"

He rolled his eyes. "How do you think Will and I got to where we are in the first place? I even told the headmistress when it began. She and a few others went to investigate but found nothing. They didn't even find strange traces of magic, and I was pretty much dismissed for having a wild imagination. Now Will's constantly breathing down my neck about it."

Perle shook her head. "Whatever it is, it doesn't seem to want to hurt us."

"Yeah, it only wants to drive *me* crazy."

"What about Zeke?"

His eyes widened. "What about him? He's just as bad as the others. Not even his wolf form could detect anything out of the ordinary among all the usual junk stored down there."

Perle rubbed her chin as she tried to make sense of his fantastic story. Maybe there was some truth to it, but she couldn't be certain. *What if there really* is *something down there threatening the school's safety?* Perle sat back in her chair and exhaled in defeat. *Not like I can do anything about it.*

Ben's gaze swiveled to her book. "That's an interesting book you got there."

"Thanks. It's a rose botany book I got from a bookseller back home. Looks like it came in handy for herbology class." She paused and glanced at the unintelligible runes written on the pages. "I just wish I knew how to read it."

Ben cocked his head. "What do you mean? The pages seem legible enough. It even has pictures."

Perle sighed. *He, too, can't see what I can see,* she thought. *Should I tell him? Would he even believe me?* Perhaps if people thought him crazy for hearing sounds in the basement, he wouldn't think she was so crazy for seeing mysterious runes in her book. "I see things in this book that apparently other people can't see," she began then explained her dilemma with the book in further detail.

His eyebrows shot up. "Amazing. What kind of runes are they? Can you draw one?" He pulled out a sheet of parchment from his bag and slid it over to her.

She looked at the blank parchment then to her open book and hesitated. "I can try…" Picking up her pen, she skimmed the open page for a random rune easy enough to draw, then she slowly transcribed it onto the parchment.

"Interesting." Ben looked thoughtfully at the parchment then eyed Perle. "And you're not enrolled in runes?"

"No. I have no idea what I drew. I just picked the easiest-looking one." *Though I should consider enrolling so I can learn how to read the rest of this book.*

"That symbol you drew means 'hand.' At least by itself."

Perle stared at him, openmouthed. "Incredible! How did you know that?"

Ben smiled broadly. "I plan on enrolling in runes next semester." His smile turned coy. "I *might* have gotten a little sneak peek of a class or two."

"You snuck into a class you weren't supposed to be in yet?"

"Eh, not the *whole* class. But enough to give me a general idea of what to expect. So, in the meantime, I've been trying to get a head start and learn a few things on my own. I recognized that rune from one of the beginner books I read recently. There are so many different meanings for the same symbol, depending on what other symbols it's paired with."

A wave of excitement and anticipation filled her. "I should start learning some basics too. Which book was it?"

"I'll go find it again. Hold on." Ben got up and headed up to the second floor, where the runic section was located.

Perle turned back to her book and exhaled. *Ben's already learning how to read runes.* Perhaps she had a hope of deciphering her mysterious book. She ran her fingers along the runes on the page. The runes gave a faint glow beneath the pads of her fingers, and she felt the symbols' faintly raised lettering from the ink. The symbols produced a warm, soothing sensation, as if reacting to her touch. Then her steady heartbeat filled her ears.

This book seems to always react to me. Is it aware of me? Is it... alive?

As if responding to her thoughts, the book emitted a bright white flash of light. Perle started, her eyes stinging a moment.

When her vision readjusted, she looked back at the book curiously. *What just happened?*

A loud thump echoed from the floor above, suddenly tearing through the library's silence. The small chandelier over her table vibrated with a high-pitched tinkle. Then Perle heard a yelp.

Perle jumped out of her chair. She looked around and noticed three students and two librarians nearby, frozen from the start. She sucked in a breath. *Ben...* She grabbed her book from the table and raced up the stairs, climbing them two by two. Reaching the top, she discovered Ben in a defensive stance, looking down one of the book aisles.

Ben whipped his head over his shoulder. "Stay back!" he called, his voice echoing off the library's ornate mahogany walls.

Two librarians on the other end of the library looked their way, their expressions dark.

Nervousness and concern filled Perle's heart. She slowly approached him, ignoring his warning. "What's going on?"

Ben huffed and looked back down the aisle, not responding. He stretched his hand toward the unseen danger.

Perle's body stiffened as she crept closer, feeling the air tense. Her heart pounded. For once, she hoped that Ben was making up a story. Pursing her lips, she peered down the long aisle of tall bookshelves.

Midway down the aisle sat a large-dog-sized red beetle. Its two glands pulsated with an eerie red glow.

Perle's eyes widened. *By the stars...*

"*De æstuspraesidio!*" Ben chanted, moving his hand in an arc. A white line formed in thin air then expanded into a translucent white light that surrounded them.

Perle gasped as she watched the light encompass them both. "What was that?"

"An elemental protection spell," Ben replied quickly and monotonously, keeping his hand outstretched. He looked deep in concentration. Faint white light continued to pulse steadily in his palm.

The beetle's glands became brighter. Perle stepped back. "What's that thing about to do?"

Ben gritted his teeth. "Get help... before that thing... torches the entire library!"

She froze, opened her mouth to scream, but no sound came out. She heard several sets of approaching footsteps. A small group of students and the two librarians rushed in their direction.

Perle looked frantically back at the beetle. *Is this thing real? Where did it come from? What is it doing here?*

The beetle crawled closer with a slow, waddling gait. A small spark of fire escaped from its mouth.

"I can't... hold this for much longer..." Ben grunted. His face contorted in pain.

She took a deep breath, trying to regain her composure. Fire in the library was never good. *Can the staff stop the thing in time? Maybe I can help somehow…*

She looked at her hands. She hadn't yet perfected her Frost Beam spell, and she hoped to the stars that her powers wouldn't fail her. She stood in front of Ben and concentrated, recalling the incantation and somatic motions and focusing those efforts on encasing the giant beetle in an icy shell. She extended her hands and chanted, *"Cicero Radium!"*

Nothing happened—her fingertips didn't so much as tingle with power. She swore under her breath. *Ugh! Of course my powers don't work when I really need them!*

The beetle exhaled a long blast of fire toward them. The fire traveled around Ben's elemental shield. Bright light surrounded them, and Perle shielded her eyes, but she felt no heat.

Ben grunted. "I'm done…" He collapsed to his knees, placed his hand on his forehead, and panted. The translucent shield disappeared.

"Stand aside!" One of the librarians hurried into the aisle and confronted the beetle. The middle-aged woman wore a long green figure-cutting robe. Cinched around her waist was an ornate gold belt inset with tiny blue jewels that glittered in the light. She moved in front of Perle and Ben, muttered something, then formed a glowing blue ball in her hands. The light became a solid, crystalline form, and the woman hurled it at the beetle. The crystals surrounded the creature, encasing it in solid ice. The throbbing glow of the beetle's glands slowed then went dark.

Perle exhaled, her heart still racing. The three students stood around them, watching, while the other librarian held a defensive stance, her outstretched hand glowing with a protection spell, which surrounded them.

"How did that creature get into the grand library?" the librarian in the green dress demanded. Affixed over her heart was a golden name tag that read "Hazel."

Perle opened her mouth to respond, noticed the cold glare in Hazel's blue eyes, and closed it.

"Fire beetles don't just appear out of thin air. Someone must have conjured one as a practical joke," Hazel continued, crossing her arms. "Which is a serious offense."

"It wasn't us." Perle gestured to herself and Ben, who was still slumped on the ground.

"I sensed the way that beetle was focused on you." Hazel pointed to Perle. "As if it was attuned to *you*."

Perle blinked. "But I didn't do it! I am not a conjurer!"

Hazel's icy-blue eyes narrowed. "We'll see what the headmistress has to say about that."

No... Perle inhaled a shaky breath. A shiver of fear raced down her back.

CHAPTER 5

PERLE'S MIND WAS SCATTERED AS she followed Hazel on a seemingly endless trek up the main building's grand staircase to the headmistress's office. *I didn't summon that thing,* she thought. Clutching her rune book in her arms, Perle looked at the back of Hazel's head. Her light-brown hair was tied in a single long braid.

While Ben had been taken to the infirmary to recover from overexerting his powers, Perle had the unfortunate luck of having to face the headmistress alone. Neither the students nor the faculty ever spoke of the headmistress by name. Perle didn't know why. She hadn't personally met the headmistress yet, and Perle wondered who she really was. She was certain the headmistress had eyes and ears all around the school, so trying to find out such secret information probably wasn't a good idea.

Is the headmistress as generous as Fairy Godmother? Perle prayed to the stars that she would be more understanding than Hazel about the library incident. *I just want to get this over with and forget this day ever happened.*

Perle followed Hazel through a set of oaken double doors into a massive room that looked about half the size of the library. Floor-to-ceiling bookshelves stretched upward toward the ornate skylight with a stained-glass image of a white pegasus. Tapestries decorated the walls, emblazoned with the school's purple-and-black crest. Two tall crystalline candelabra flanked an ornate mahogany desk, casting their gleaming light across the wood floor. A gold nameplate that read "Headmistress" sat on one corner of the desk, while a shiny bright-red apple sat on the other corner. The high-backed chair was turned around, facing the large, arched window behind the desk.

Perle took a deep breath. Despite the numerous old books everywhere, the room had a pleasant floral smell.

Hazel stopped in front of the desk and inclined her head. "Headmistress, there was a situation in the library today that could use your input."

Perle lowered her head and wrung her hands. *What's going to happen to me?* she wondered.

The desk chair swiveled around slowly, and Perle looked up at a petite woman with smooth, flawless fair skin, rosy cheeks, and full ruby-red lips. A small red bow was neatly tied in her short ebony hair. Perle's jaw dropped slowly. That's *the headmistress? She's beautiful!*

The headmistress's light-brown eyes met Perle's, and she smiled warmly. Then she acknowledged Hazel. "So I've heard," she said in a soft, endearing voice.

Perle stared. The woman seemed like a pure angel of goodness. *Or is it all a disguise?*

"A fire beetle in the library is most disturbing." The headmistress studied Perle with curious eyes. "But to my understanding, Ms. Durand, you are taking evocation classes, yes?"

Perle was about to ask how she knew that when she realized the silliness of the question. *Of course, she probably knows the details of every student here.* "Oui, Headmistress," she confirmed with a nod. Though, she already dreaded that she'd completely missed that day's class, thanks to the library incident. "I don't know how that creature got into the library."

Hazel's gaze whipped back and forth between Perle and the headmistress, then her jaw clenched. "That creature was attuned to Ms. Durand! I felt it clearly! She was directly involved in this incident. Mr. Spriggan was also present, but he became incapacitated after overexerting himself spellcasting."

The headmistress's gaze filled with concern. "Is he all right?" she asked, her soft smile faltering.

"Yes, he is recovering now in the infirmary," Hazel confirmed.

"That's good news." The headmistress tapped her chin in thought. "I sincerely hope that fire beetle wasn't trying to become Ms. Durand's familiar. That would be most troublesome."

A familiar? Perle was aware of such phenomena happening to certain people who held a special kind of magical power. At least, that was how she understood it. Some people were able to magically bond with a creature, while others were not. A number of factors were involved in the process, but it all came down to mere chance of making the right bond, which one could spend their entire life trying to find. Perle's parents, as magically gifted as they were, had never found such bonds, and Perle assumed there would be no chance for her either. "I don't think it was trying to become my familiar, Headmistress." Perle shook her head. "It was breathing fire at me. I tried to stop it, but my powers failed me."

The headmistress's full lips pressed into a thin ruby-red line. She gave a dismissive nod to Hazel. "Please leave us. I need to speak with Ms. Durand in private."

Hazel opened her mouth as if to say something more, but then she quickly closed it. She exhaled through her nose and spun on her heel. "Yes, of course, Headmistress."

Perle stepped aside as Hazel marched to the door. When she was gone, Perle looked upon the headmistress once more.

The kindly woman beckoned her closer to her desk with a wave of her slender hand. "Come closer, Perle."

Perle hesitated when she heard the headmistress address her by her first name. But she heard no malice or anger in the woman's voice, so she approached with slow, cautious steps.

The headmistress studied her, tilting her head. Then her eyes lowered to the book in Perle's arms. "What is that you have there?"

"This?" Perle showed her the rune book. "It's just a rose botany book I brought from home. I was using it to study for one of my herbology assignments." She decided it was best not to mention the runes and further complicate matters. *She'll think I'm seeing things if I try to explain, anyway,* she figured.

The woman's warm smile returned. "I see. Well, I'm sure it was all a bit unsettling at the library. I do believe you that you didn't summon that creature, but I am also inclined to agree with Hazel's assessment of the creature trying to bond with you. I can sense your unique power— compassion, determination, willingness— qualities that any magical creature would be attracted to."

Perle exhaled a small breath of relief when the headmistress didn't question her about the book further. She clutched the book to her chest and felt a soothing warmth emanate from it and spread through her body. Her smile faltered, and she swiveled her gaze to the book. *Is it... reacting to me?* she wondered.

She noticed, from the corner of her eye, the headmistress hold up her hand. The woman's index finger lifted slightly toward a wooden perch near a bookshelf. A tiny bluebird that sat upon the perch flew down and landed gracefully on the headmistress's finger. The bird trilled a happy song and ruffled its feathers.

"This is Azure, my bonded companion," the headmistress continued, inching her hand closer to Perle. "One day, when I was very young, I went for a walk in the woods. I sat down to rest, and that was when he came to greet me and keep me company with his beautiful songs. We haven't been apart since."

Perle smiled at the touching story, a hint of sadness filling her heart, as she knew she would most likely never be so fortunate. "He's beautiful."

Azure tweeted another song in response.

Perle watched the bird carefully then tilted her head. *He must be a pretty old bird to have been with her this long. Yet, he still looks so vibrant and young.* "How old is he?" she asked.

"Actually, he's ageless. With the magical bond that we share, he continues to live for as long as I do," the headmistress explained.

"Interesting."

"Indeed. And as for you, dear Perle, there may be hope for you yet to bond with a familiar of your own. But such things can take time."

Perle shook her head. "I doubt anything will want to bond with me until I learn to control my powers. I'm still struggling with one of the beginning assignments in evocation class." She spotted an apple-shaped clock hanging on the wall behind the desk, which confirmed her suspicion that she had already missed her class. She sighed.

The headmistress lifted an eyebrow. "I would recommend you find more time to visit the practice chambers to perfect your assignments. That's what they're for, after all."

Perle nodded once. *All I ever wanted was to be in control, so I'll do whatever it takes.* "*Merci*, Headmistress. I will do my best and work harder," she said.

"That's all I ever ask of my students. I'm curious, however. Which spells have you perfected so far?"

Perle felt her cheeks get hot. It was embarrassing to think that the only spell she'd managed to master was a cantrip so basic that even a toddler could cast it in its sleep. "Uh… just the Light spell…" she said in a small voice.

"That's good. It's a most useful spell." The headmistress nodded approvingly.

She can't be serious…

"Now, then," the woman continued. "As for the beetle incident, I will see that the matter is investigated further and find out how it was conjured." She stood from her desk, revealing a long, flowing dark-blue dress that gently hugged her thin frame. "That is all for now. You're dismissed."

Perle blinked. *That's it? I'm not in trouble?* "A-are you sure, Headmistress?"

"Of course. I don't believe you would jeopardize the safety of this school. You have a pure heart. Something is amiss around here, and I intend to get to the bottom of it soon enough." She waved her hand dismissively. "Go on, now, while I prepare for my next appointment."

Perle let out a deep sigh. Relief spread through her body like a wave, easing her fast-beating heart. "*Merci. Merci,* Headmistress!" Perle clasped her hands and bowed repeatedly to the woman as she backed away from the desk.

The woman's polite smile broadened, her eyes narrowing in delight, and she waved.

Perle hurried out of the office. She leaned her back against the closed door and sighed. *She's truly the most beautiful and generous person I've ever met,* she thought. It was good to know that she would be cleared from the beetle mess.

A deep animal growl rumbled nearby. Perle pushed off the door with a start and whipped her head to the source of the familiar gruff sound. Zeke sat in a chair in the waiting area, glaring back at her.

Perle bit her bottom lip. "H-hi, Zeke," she said in a small voice.

Zeke grunted. "What did the headmistress want with you?"

Perle opened her mouth to reply then quickly closed it. She was surprised that he was actually talking to her more, even if he'd only asked a simple question. "N-nothing special. She just wanted to talk to me about my evocation class."

He sniffed, lifted his head, and narrowed his eyes. "You're lying."

Perle shook her head quickly. "N-no, I'm not." She backed away from him slowly. The last thing she wanted was to make him angry in front of the headmistress's office. "Why are you here?"

"Hmph. I'm here because the headmistress summoned me. I have to report back to her every so often. She gave me a… special assignment."

Perle furrowed her brow. *Special assignment?* Curiosity swarmed her mind as she wondered what sort of assignment it could be. She decided not to prod any further about his business. "I see. Well, um, I have to get to class now. *Salut.*"

Zeke growled again.

She raced down the stairs, not looking back, praying to the stars that she wouldn't be pursued.

CHAPTER 6

AFTER A QUICK STOP AT the infirmary to check on Ben, who was already gone, Perle raced back to her dorm. She shut the door behind her and leaned against it, panting. With the headmistress excusing her from evocation class, Perle decided to confine herself in the dorm for the rest of the day.

She had the place to herself, with Anala away at her afternoon flight class. The mouthwatering aroma of Anala's ratatouille permeated the entire suite. Perle planted herself at the tiny table in the kitchenette and enjoyed a bowl of the warm stew. It wasn't quite as amazing as her father's, but it was still delicious, enough for Perle to get seconds. She returned to the table and pored over her botany-turned-rune book. She was starting to notice a pattern. Her parents and Ben saw legible writing about roses on the pages whereas Perle only saw runes. *Is this book cognizant of me? What's the enchantment involved?* she wondered.

Perle sighed at the endless pages of runes that stared back at her mockingly. She wished she could read them as well as Ben. Even recognizing a handful of runes would be progress. *If I could read this book, then maybe I would be able to understand and control my powers more, and maybe next time I would be able to protect people in danger.*

A furious knock suddenly echoed from the front door. Perle jumped. Her bottom was sore, and glancing at the dragon-silhouette-shaped wall clock, she realized almost two hours had passed. Dinner would soon start in the dining hall. *Who could be visiting me now?*

"Perle? You there?" Ben's muffled voice was followed by another series of knocks.

Perle deflated, relief spreading through her to know that Ben was okay. She rushed to the door. "Ben?"

"It's happening again."

The elation suddenly turned to dread. *Another beetle?* She hesitated to open the door. "Ugh. Please don't tell me there's another—"

"The basement. The sounds are back."

She remembered the confrontation earlier between Ben and Will about the strange sounds that Ben had heard. "Does anyone else know about this?"

"You're the only one I've told because you're the only one who'll believe me. Let me show you."

She heaved a deep sigh, flaring her nostrils. Then she finally flung open the door.

Ben stood, his jaw rigid. "The cries in the basement are even louder now."

She pursed her lips. "No tricks, Ben."

He shook his head. "I wouldn't joke around about something like this." He made a small head gesture for her to follow him.

Clutching her book under one arm, Perle followed Ben down to the main floor of the dormitory. A buzz of murmurs floated around from the few students who occupied the atrium.

"When did they let you out of the infirmary?" Perle asked as they detoured down a narrow hallway lit dimly by strategically placed wall sconces.

"Eh, less than fifteen minutes after I arrived," Ben said. "I was told to return to my dorm and rest for the remainder of the day. Thankfully, I had already finished my classes for the day."

"What you did back there at the library was amazing."

He slowed his steps and turned his head slightly over his shoulder. "It was all I could do. I'm just glad all that practicing worked. What happened to you after I was toted away to the infirmary?"

Perle stopped, briefly averting her gaze. Then she gave him a brief recount of her meeting with the headmistress.

"Well, it's a relief that she didn't think you were the one who conjured the beetle." Ben pointed to a closed door with a gold sign affixed that read, "Storage Area. Authorized Personnel Only!"

"This leads to the basement?" she asked. Her arm cradling the book suddenly tingled with a strange, warm sensation. She became more aware of her surroundings, as if she felt like she was being watched, but as she looked around, she saw nothing. She slowly approached the door and placed her ear to it. She waited a few moments until she heard it, a high-pitched cry. She gasped, widened her eyes, and pulled back from the door. "Ah… is someone trapped down there?"

Ben shook his head solemnly. "I don't know."

"Let's tell Zeke or one of the other RAs."

"I told you before, I did, and nothing came of it."

"The headmistress?" She swallowed, hesitant to suggest it.

"Tried that too. No one sees the headmistress without an appointment unless overridden by one of the faculty. By the time all of that's arranged, the sounds are pretty much gone."

Perle rubbed her chin. "Maybe whatever's down there isn't some*one* but some*thing*." She thought about her recent conversation with the headmistress. "Ben, do you have a familiar?"

He snorted. "I wish."

"If you're the only one who's been able to hear the sounds, then maybe whatever's down there is trying to bond with you."

A hopeful smile crept onto his lips. "You think so?"

"There's only one way to find out, but..." She looked at the conspicuous sign on the door.

Ben pursed his lips. "I'm sure the faculty wouldn't punish me for finding whatever it is down there that's trying to bond with me, right?"

She cringed. *I guess it wouldn't hurt to take a peek down there. Though I still can't shake the feeling that we're being watched. Does the headmistress already know?* She tried the door, but as she suspected, it was locked.

"I'll get that." Ben brushed past her. He revealed a silver key from his pocket.

Perle blinked. "You had a key to the basement all this time?"

Ben cringed. "No… I sort of borrowed it from the groundskeeper's office while he was away on his lunch break today. But you can't just open this door with the key alone. You have to use it in conjunction with the right spell, which can only be cast by abjurers."

"You *stole* the key from the groundskeeper?"

"No! *Borrowed.* I'm going to put it back after we're done here."

She flared her nostrils. *How in the stars did I get myself into this mess?* "If the headmistress ever finds out about this, we'll both be in trouble."

"We'll be done before she or anyone else finds out," he assured. "Let's just get in there, look around, and leave." He stuck the key in the lock and placed his other hand on the door, and as he turned the key, he uttered an incoherent phrase. His hand emitted a yellow glow, which transferred to the knob. Perle heard a subtle click, and the door creaked open.

Perle raised her eyebrows. "How did you know how to do that? You seem like you've done this before."

Ben shook his head. "Nope. I watched the groundskeeper do it when I came down here the first time with him and the headmistress. I didn't realize he was an abjurer until he cast a spell that opens locks."

Perle nodded and directed her attention to the basement stairs descending into blackness. A whiff of musty, stale air wafted to her nostrils, and she wrinkled her nose. Though she still couldn't hear voices, she sensed something was amiss.

"Do you have a light?" Ben asked.

A light... she perked up. *Of course!* The only cantrip she was confident about casting was at her fingertips. She looked around for an object to apply the spell to and decided to use her book. Grasping the book with both hands, Perle closed her eyes and concentrated, tapping into the inner threads of her magical essence in the same manner she recalled from her last evocation lecture. "*Lux*," she whispered.

Moments later, a tingling sensation spread through her hands, then they went alight. The light transferred to the book, and it emitted a soft white glow that created a large circle of illumination around Perle and Ben and tapered off into the blackness as it stretched farther down the stairs.

"Excellent!" Ben hissed. He nodded to her. "Lead the way."

Perle descended the stairs, the light from the book illuminating her path. Her heart raced as she slowly proceeded into the unknown depths. She still didn't hear any sounds. Part of her wanted to turn back, but Ben was close behind her, and she knew he wouldn't let the mystery go unsolved.

They reached the bottom of the stairs, and the basement door creaked eerily closed.

Perle jumped and whirled around. "Did you do that?" she asked Ben before swiveling her gaze up the stairs.

"Not me." He scratched the back of his head, his eyes swiveling sideways.

Perle took another deep breath to regain her composure. "Right. Well, let's look around." She held the book out in front of her and illuminated an area full of stacked wooden crates and bins filled with cleaning supplies.

Something light skittered across the floor, making her cringe. Her skin prickled. "Ugh! What was that?"

"We're in a dark basement. I'm sure it's pest heaven down here."

"After dealing with that beetle, I don't want to see any more pests."

Ben chuckled.

A high-pitched cry echoed from behind one of the crates. Perle froze at the familiar noise. *It can't be!*

"There it is again!" Ben whispered, pointing toward the sound.

Something small, black, and furry crawled out from behind the boxes.

Perle widened her eyes. "Nuit?" The book dropped from her hands, landing with a loud thump.

Nuit jumped and cowered behind the boxes again, then meowed. He poked his head around the corner, the light from the book reflecting a hazy golden grey from the cat's eyes.

Perle rushed over and scooped up her pet, cuddling him in her arms. "What a surprise!"

"Wait... that's what's been making all that noise? And it's yours?" Ben looked dumbfounded.

"Oui." She held Nuit at eye level. "How did you get here?"

Nuit meowed and licked the tip of her nose.

Perle sighed and looked at Ben. "This is very odd. I didn't bring him with me when I arrived." She bit her bottom lip. "Do you think the headmistress will let me keep him?"

Ben rubbed his chin. "Maybe. If you tell her he's your familiar, she might."

Perle cringed. "She'll know he's not. He's just a pet, not a familiar."

"Hey, I'm just glad this mystery was solved. It was your cat all along." Ben narrowed his eyes and approached one of the walls. He moved a crate aside and knelt behind it. "This must be how he got in here."

Curious, Perle followed him and discovered a hole at the bottom of the wall that was big enough for a small animal to fit through. A dim red-orange beam of light from the early-evening sunset poured in through the hole.

"That hole's hiding in plain sight," Ben continued. "Who knows what else is down here because of it?"

"We should let Zeke know," Perle suggested.

"Eh, bad idea." Ben scrunched his nose.

"Why? As an RA, he can see to it that the wall is fixed."

"Not before he interrogates us about why we were down here in the first place." Ben shook his hand dismissively. "Look. I'd rather not get on his bad side twice in one day."

"Then who should we tell?"

Ben rubbed his chin. "How about you find a way to get an appointment with the headmistress and tell her you found your familiar."

She blinked. "And when she finds out it was all a lie?"

"Then just say it was an honest mistake." He shrugged. "Look, we'll deal with this, so stop worrying. At least you're reunited with your cat, right?"

She looked at Nuit, who was purring in her arms, his eyes half-closed in contentment. *As long as the headmistress doesn't make me give you up,* she thought. "Fine." She looked back at Ben. "You just better know what you're doing."

She knelt to pick up her dropped book from the ground, when it suddenly gave off a blinding white flash. Nuit hissed and jumped out of her arms as she shielded her face. The light dissipated, and Perle took a moment for her vision to adjust to the basement's dimness.

Out of the corner of her eye, she noticed one of the crates of old books shift. Then something large and green whisked out from the darkness and approached. It reached the outer ring of light, which outlined the tiny hairs on the massive, outstretched legs of a giant, human-sized spider. Its many eyes glowed a deep crimson.

Perle screamed and jumped back.

"Whoa!" Ben exclaimed, joining her. "When I said there were pests down here, I didn't think it would be pests *that* huge."

"Just… get rid of it!" Perle shrieked.

"*De æstuspraesidio!*" Ben chanted, activating his elemental protection spell. His gaze focused toward the creature, and his hand extended in front of him. "Your turn," he said to Perle.

Perle flared her nostrils in frustration. *My turn for what? Another failed spell?* Unlike before, at the library, they were alone, and the spider looked ready to have the two of them for dinner. She balled her hands into fists and looked at them. *Don't fail me again, please…* She inhaled deeply through her nose and unclenched her hands. Turning to the spider, she held out her hands, concentrating on the Frost Beam spell she had been desperately trying to perfect. "*Cicero Radium!*" she whispered, but somewhere in the back of her mind, she felt uneasy. That feeling of being watched rattled her nerves.

Her fingers tingled, but nothing happened. Perle swore under her breath.

A guttural growl suddenly echoed from the shadows. Perle froze, her gaze darting about the darkness beyond the ring of light. A large, shadowed outline zipped past her faster than she could blink. The shadow appeared behind the spider and loomed. The ring of light revealed a large grey wolf with glowing yellow eyes.

"Oh great..." Ben muttered through clenched teeth.

The wolf bared its canines. The hair on the back of its neck flared up like spikes.

"*A wolf!*" Perle yelped. "Look out, Ben!" She grabbed the back of Ben's shirt and pulled him away from the wolf and spider.

"Ugh!" Ben stumbled and lost his concentration, causing his elemental protection spell to falter. His eyes flashed a hazy white then returned to normal. The translucent white shield of light that surrounded them disappeared.

"Get it together," Perle said to Ben, noticing the slight look of exhaustion on his face. "Now we have two things to worry about." She pointed to the spider and the wolf.

The wolf growled at them then faced the hissing spider.

The spider skittered away from the wolf, out of the ring of light, and toward the stairs. The wolf snarled and pursued it. The wolf leapt toward the spider, and they tumbled into the outer fringes of darkness, where Perle could barely make out the two figures tussling and rolling about. A pair of spindly legs wrapped around the wolf's silhouette. A series of snarls, growls, and hisses followed, and finally a weak howl. The wolf snapped its jaws at the spider, and the creature let out a hiss. The spindly legs released the wolf, and the spider disappeared. The wolf hobbled backward, let out a howl of pain, then collapsed in the darkness. All was quiet.

Perle's heart pounded. She exchanged glances with Ben, her mind spinning with questions.

Ben pursed his lips. "I'll check it out."

"Wait." Perle took a deep breath and picked up the book. "You won't see anything without this. We'll go together."

With the book providing a lit path, Perle and Ben carefully approached the stairs. There, they discovered the spider, which lay dead in a pool of a sickly green slimy-looking substance, its hairy legs crinkled around its mutilated body. The light stretched far enough to illuminate part of a man's hand stretched out next to the spider. Cringing, Perle moved the light over the hand connected to the familiar-looking man with short grey-streaked black hair, who lay naked and deathly still.

CHAPTER 7

ZEKE... PERLE CHEWED HER BOTTOM lip as she paced back and forth in the waiting area outside the infirmary. It was almost midnight. Her mind still spun, reliving the horrific encounter in the basement earlier that evening. While Ben had run to get help, Perle reluctantly stayed at Zeke's side, hoping and praying to the stars that he would be okay. Awkward didn't begin to describe the way she'd felt as she'd kept watch over Zeke, who had lain completely naked after his shifting. She could only imagine how problematic—not to mention embarrassing—it had to be for him if his clothes got destroyed every time he shifted. She wondered if Anala had the same problem, being a dragon shifter. Perle had yet to see her in her true form— for which Perle was grateful.

Once Zeke had been safely transported to the infirmary, Perle made a quick stop at her dorm to drop off her book as well as keep Nuit out of sight. To her relief, Anala wasn't around to give her the third degree.

The brass knob of the infirmary's door jiggled. Perle stopped pacing, turning her attention to the sound. A woman poked her head out. A gold name tag that read "Berri" was affixed over the breast of her flowing white dress. A pair of translucent blue butterfly wings fluttered behind her. Bright-blue glitter rained from them and disappeared before it hit the floor. Her smooth, creamy face was expressionless.

Perle regarded the blue faerie with trepidation. "Is he—"

Berri held up her slender hand, silencing Perle. "He's lucky he got here when he did. He was severely poisoned from the spider bite on his neck. I've not seen a case like this in many years. Only a few species of spiders are so toxic to shifters."

Relief surged through Perle. "I am glad he's okay. May I see him?"

"Yes, and will you also describe that spider to me again? I finally found the arachnology book I was looking for earlier." Berri held up a small, thick tome in one hand while she opened the door for Perle with the other.

Perle hesitated and looked into the large, bright room that echoed with the hums and fizzles of numerous magical crystals, orbs, tubes, and other strange devices. Zeke lay in one of the few occupied recovery beds, a large green crystal floating beside him. Green energy surged from the crystal and encompassed him in a pulsing, glowing light that gave off a gentle, soothing hum.

He saved us, Perle thought. She grabbed her satchel from the chair and entered the infirmary. The brash, mysterious man who garnered fear from everyone was willing to risk his life for someone he barely knew. Somehow, she felt secure just being in his presence.

"I've never seen such a large spider before," Perle told Berri as they walked together. "It was green, hairy, and had vicious, glowing red eyes."

Berri stopped and flipped through the pages of her book. "Red eyes that glow…" Her eyes widened, and her wings quivered nervously. "By the stars! According to this, you found an arachnea, a creature that can only be summoned by a special spell."

Perle's jaw dropped. *A magical spider? Like the fire beetle?* Her heart pounded. *Who or what is summoning them?*

"Are you sure that's the spider you saw?" Berri showed her the page with an illustration of the creature. Sure enough, it looked exactly the same as Perle remembered.

Perle nodded slowly. "Oui, but I swear, I have no knowledge of such a spell."

Berri's face hardened, and she shut the book. "I didn't think you did. The spell is highly advanced, nothing that any of the undergraduates would be capable of performing. There is something amiss around here, and I don't like it."

Whoever was behind it, Perle wondered if she was the target—or maybe Ben. So far, it had seemed like the magical creatures appeared while the two of them were together.

The light hum of a nearby floating healing crystal reminded Perle of why she was there. She approached Zeke's bedside and stopped. Berri stood on the other side of the bed, her rapidly batting wings slowing to a calm flutter.

Perle stared at Zeke's peaceful face as he slept. The bedcovers gently rose and lowered steadily with each breath he took. Wisps of his silver-grey hair draped across his face. She absently reached out, intending to brush the strands away, when he grabbed her hand. She flinched.

Zeke's eyelids shot open. He focused on her for a moment, then his upper lip curled. A low growl rumbled in his throat. The bedside crystal's green light disappeared.

Berri gasped. "No sudden movements, Mr. Wolfson!" She rested her hand across his forehead, and a soft blue light radiated from her palm.

Zeke calmed, releasing Perle's hand. The crystal's green light returned and encompassed his body with a slow, pulsating glow. His eyes remained on Perle. One corner of his mouth twitched.

Perle wrung her hands. "Ah... *m-merci*, Zeke, for saving me and Ben. I know my words probably don't mean much, seeing as you risked your life for us."

"That spider should've bitten Ben instead," Zeke snarled.

"Don't say such things about your peers, Mr. Wolfson," Berri said.

"But that fool led Perle right into danger!"

Perle heard the hint of concern in his voice, and her heart stuttered. *Zeke was worried about me?*

"That is a matter for the headmistress to deal with," Berri said. "But right now, we're talking about you, Mr. Wolfson. The headmistress put a lot of faith in you when she appointed you as an RA. You need to have regard for *all* your peers, no matter who they are."

Perle sucked in a breath. *His role as an RA is the headmistress's doing?* She wondered how he'd earned such a position. *Had he done something extraordinary for the headmistress, as he'd done for me and Ben?*

Zeke gritted his teeth. "None of this would've happened if *certain people* hadn't gone into the basement in the first place." He cast a dark gaze at Perle.

Perle felt her heart thump as she realized she had become the subject of the conversation. "I agreed to go down there to investigate the sounds that Ben claimed he'd kept hearing. It turned out to be my cat, Nuit. It's my fault. I should've been the one sent to the headmistress's office, not Ben."

Zeke's eyebrows rose slightly. "Why? I saw the whole thing. He coerced you into going into the basement, and I'm going to inform the groundskeeper of Ben's little stunt once I'm out of here."

Perle sighed, her suspicions confirmed of the feeling she'd felt earlier. *So, he was watching us the whole time.* "Don't… please," she said in a small voice. "He's already in enough trouble with the headmistress."

Zeke's eyebrows rose slightly.

"What *I* want to know is," Berri interjected, pinning her gaze on Perle, "who put such a dangerous creature in the basement?"

"I don't know, but there was a hole in the wall," Perle explained. "It led right outside. That must be how Nuit got in."

Berri shook her head. "You have one lucky cat for it to have survived so long with an arachnea and not become that creature's dinner."

Perle shivered at the thought of Nuit becoming the spider's next meal.

"The school is in danger. I must alert the headmistress at once." Berri turned to leave.

Zeke grunted and sat up in bed. "Can I go now? I feel fine."

Berri turned her attention back to him and placed her hand on his shoulder in a reassuring gesture. "The poison may not be completely out of your system. I know you shifters have fast healing, but it's best you remain under observation for a day, at least."

Zeke growled. "I said I'm fine. I don't have time to lie around for a whole day. If this place is in danger, then I need to do my job and help protect my peers."

Berri pursed her lips. Then she reached into a cabinet next to the bed and retrieved a tiny glass vial containing a light-green liquid. "If you feel even the *slightest* sign of a relapse, take this immediately. All of it."

Zeke took the vial from Berri and looked at it. After Berri left, Zeke wrapped the bedsheets around his waist and rolled out of bed. The green light from his bedside healing crystal disappeared again. He stood before Perle, his tall, athletic build looming over her.

Perle's heart thrummed. Heat rushed to her cheeks as she was struck by his dashing brown eyes, in which she sensed a hint of concern. *Was he really worried about me?* she wondered, averting her gaze. "Merci again, Zeke." She turned toward the exit. "I… should go see if Ben is okay."

Zeke let out a low snarl. "Why? He put you in danger."

"It wasn't deliberate. We didn't know what we'd find in the basement. Besides, I agreed to go with him."

"He was feeding you wild stories."

"The stories were true. He heard sounds, and they turned out to be my cat." She paused and narrowed her eyes. "Say, don't wolves have a keen sense of smell? How come you didn't smell Nuit down there when you investigated the basement the first time?"

Zeke scowled. "There are a lot of things—a lot of mixed scents like bugs, old clothes, cleaning supplies, and more—in the basement, which make it difficult to pinpoint a single one. And your cat could have been outside at the time I went down there, which wouldn't make things any easier."

She nodded once, though her heart still stung that Zeke was upset about Ben. She lifted her head and hardened her gaze. "Look, Ben's not a bad person. He was trying to warn everyone, but no one would believe him, no one but me."

He blinked. "But—"

"An RA's job is to listen to their peers, no? Maybe you should do that before making accusations." Mixed feelings surged through her fast-beating heart. *Did I just say that to him?* She mentally swore for letting her feelings overtake her rationale.

Zeke opened his mouth then closed it. His face darkened with rage.

The air grew tense. Not wanting to rile Zeke any further, she spun on her heel and marched out of the infirmary. She pressed her back against the closed door. Balling her fists, she thought about their conversation. *He has no idea about Ben. No one seems to understand him. No one but me...*

She pushed off the door and started down the dark, empty hall. The infirmary door burst open again. She spun around.

Zeke stood in the doorway, glaring. "You can't see Ben."

Perle exhaled. "Why not? What gives you the right to tell me who I can and can't see?"

"Because it's after hours, and I'm in charge around here. Lights out. I suggest you return to your dorm and get some sleep."

She blinked. "Are you serious? How can I sleep at a time like this?"

Zeke took a deep breath. His muscles relaxed, and his brown eyes regarded her with a hint of compassion. "Look, I'll check on Ben in his dorm. I'm sure the headmistress dismissed him hours ago. I'll let you know how he's doing."

She could hear the sincerity in his words, which eased her tension and anger, but she still wasn't sure about him. "Do you promise?"

He bristled. "When I say I'll do something, I do it."

She pursed her lips and reluctantly nodded. "Merci."

He stepped closer to her. "And tomorrow, I'll get to the bottom of this mystery."

The warmth of his closeness made her skin prickle with goosebumps. *He plans to figure it out alone?* "Let me help," she said.

"No. It's my job as an RA to look after my peers. I'll do it."

She felt compelled to retort but decided against it. "Very well. *Salut*, Zeke…" She gave him a small wave and continued down the hall without looking back. However, her heart wouldn't stop pounding as she thought about the intent way he'd looked at her when they'd been standing close. And even as she was halfway down the hall, she could still feel him watching her.

These summoned creatures seem to be targeting me and Ben, she thought. *Maybe it'll be easier for me to try to find some clues on how to stop it.* She made a plan to begin her investigations after evocation class the following day. Hopefully, her rune book, which remained safely in her room, would help her uncover some clues.

CHAPTER 8

PERLE COULDN'T FOCUS ON THE current lesson in evocation class. She'd barely gotten any sleep after yesterday's incident. She was worried at the thought of more giant creatures lurking around the academy, ready to claim an unsuspecting student as their next meal.

Zeke's already handling it, Perle thought. She glanced at her botany book peeking out from her open satchel on the floor next to her and the small slip of paper that bookmarked one of the pages. She smiled at the paper, which Zeke had slipped under her door earlier that morning. It was a note, written in his scrawling handwriting, about Ben. As Zeke had promised, he'd checked on Ben, who was all right, but that didn't stop the idea that the creatures might be attracted to her from plaguing her heart.

"Ms. Durand, please demonstrate the somatic gestures of the Fire Hands spell."

Perle stood eye to eye with her evocation professor, Mistress Jorinda Fitcher. The thin, brown-haired, middle-aged woman looked down her nose at Perle with expectant emerald eyes.

Perle swallowed. *Ugh. I should've been paying attention.* She glanced at the few notes she'd jotted down, but nothing related to the current lecture. Raking her fingers though her hair, she looked up and realized all eyes were focused on her. She grimaced. "Ah…"

Mistress Fitcher's expression hardened. "You *have* been paying attention, yes?"

Perle cleared her throat and stood up from her chair. "Oui, of course." She slowly made her way to the center of the room and stood before the large, gaudy metallic dummy that was used for demonstrating spells. *Why would she call on me for this?* she wondered. She'd utterly and completely failed the execution of her Frost Beam spell earlier, unlike the rest of her peers. It seemed she was set for another round of public embarrassment.

Sighing, she stood before the dummy. She wiggled her fingers awkwardly, concentrating on the fire element, but the warm sensation never came to her hands. She deflated.

"Wrong. All wrong," Mistress Fitcher scolded. "Two fingers pointing up, and rotate them counterclockwise in a vertical position, from top to bottom. Try again."

Perle took another breath, staring at the dummy with more determination. She closed her eyes a moment, concentrated on the somatic components of each movement, and opened them again. *I see it now.* Something sparked in her mind as her task became clearer. She held two fingers in front of her, focusing on a tiny vital spot marked between the dummy's eyes. "*Manibus ignis...*" Moving her hands slowly, she concentrated again. Heat rose from her body and channeled up toward her fingers. Her vision became infused with a fiery-orange hue. The world around her wavered from her heated aura. Flames appeared around her hands, then a stream of fire shot from her fingers toward the dummy, hitting its mark perfectly between the eyes. The force of the blast jerked the dummy backward, its stability base preventing it from falling over completely.

The magical sensation ebbed from her body as Perle observed her results. She quirked a smile. *I did it!*

"Well done, Ms. Durand." Mistress Fitcher nodded. Then she addressed the rest of the students. "Take notes, class. It's imperative that you focus precisely on your target before attempting this spell. Your assignment tonight will be to memorize and perfect this spell. We will be having an exam next class, and you'll be required to cast Frost Beam and Fire Hands flawlessly. Class dismissed."

As Perle returned to her desk to retrieve her bag, Mistress Fitcher stopped her. "You're still struggling in some areas, but I appreciate that you're not giving up. Most students in your situation would have done so by now."

Perle frowned. It didn't help that she'd been distracted all day, but she dared not tell Mistress Fitcher that. "Merci."

"That's all that matters. Now, imagine your capabilities if your mind were clear and focused?" She gave Perle a pointed look.

Perle averted her gaze. *Ugh, she was already onto me...* "I'll do my best, Mistress."

"Do more than your best, Ms. Durand." Mistress Fitcher lifted her chin. "Excel."

With a sigh, Perle gathered her belongings and left the lecture hall. She observed the other students scrambling throughout the crowded halls. Thankfully, she was finished with classes for the day, which gave her time to begin her investigation. She decided to start at the library, where the problem began.

As Perle reached the library's double doors, a bright-blue bird landed on her shoulder. She started and looked at the familiar bird. "Azure? Where did you come from?" she asked.

The bird whistled a fanciful song, bobbing his tail.

Perle tilted her head as she tried to make sense of what the bird was saying. The bird whistled again, and suddenly, Perle heard a familiar voice in her mind.

"Please report to my office, Ms. Durand."

Perle gasped at the headmistress's voice, which sounded so close. She looked around frantically, but the woman was nowhere to be found. She looked at Azure again. "Did—did you say that?"

The bluebird gave another whistle and flew out the open door, where students continuously came and went.

Perle dragged her feet back to the headmistress's office and stared at the shut oaken doors. Her mind swarmed with thoughts about what the headmistress would want with her. *Did she somehow find out about my intentions to investigate the source of the mysterious creatures?* Perle wondered. The headmistress probably wouldn't let her off easy like before. If the creatures were targeting Perle, then her presence was a threat to the entire school. *It's probably best that I leave rather than endanger anyone else.*

She reached for the brass handle, and the doors swung open on their own. The headmistress sat at her desk, her white quill pen moving quickly as she scribbled something.

Perle waited a few moments for the headmistress to acknowledge her, but the woman didn't look up from her work. Her quill pen moved steadily back and forth. Perle took a breath, lowered her head, and stepped inside. The doors closed behind her with an echoing clang that reverberated throughout the office, and the sound of the rapid scribbling stopped.

"Ah, good afternoon, Ms. Durand." The headmistress set down her pen and gestured to the high-backed executive chairs in front of her desk. "Please."

Perle swallowed then slowly drew closer. She looked around, wondering if she was truly alone with the headmistress. She glanced above the desk at the perch where Azure was preening himself. She hesitantly set down her satchel, slid into one of the chairs, and clasped her hands in her lap.

"Please don't be alarmed. You're not in trouble or anything. I just wanted to discuss some things with you," the headmistress assured her.

She straightened in her chair, a small breath of relief escaping her chest.

"Mr. Spriggan filled me in on what happened in the basement. Though the matter is still under investigation, I have no doubts that neither of you are the cause of the disturbance."

"Ah, merci. I am so grateful that you believe us." Perle clasped her hands.

The headmistress nodded. "Yes, however, the matter I wanted to discuss with you specifically has to do with the cat that was found—*your* cat."

Her nerves returned as she thought about Nuit, whom she'd kept safely confined in her suite for the time being. She was aware of the rules. No pets allowed, only familiars. And even then, they had to be approved by the school. "I'm sorry, Headmistress. I had no intentions of bringing Nuit here. He's my pet, not a familiar, unfortunately."

The headmistress raised her eyebrows. "Are you sure about that?"

"Absolutely. He must've stowed away in my carriage on the ride here and somehow found his way to the basement and stayed there that entire time. Thank the stars he wasn't eaten by that giant spider."

"So, you're saying your cat, Nuit, ran away from home just to be with you?"

"Oui. That's what it seems like."

"Have you thought about Nuit since you arrived?"

Perle furrowed her brow. *What kind of question is that?* she thought. "Of course. There was never a time I wasn't thinking about what he was up to while I wasn't home, if he missed me."

A small smile parted the woman's lips. "He's more intelligent than the average cat to have come all this way with you and found such a discreet place to hide just to be near you."

"We've been inseparable since my father found him alone as a small kitten. He's never gotten very big and still has kitten-like tendencies. He also likes to talk to me. Well, he tries to, anyway. Sometimes when I'm sad, he seems to know and does little things to cheer me up, like roll on his back or make cute little cat sounds."

The headmistress chuckled. "Well, it certainly sounds like he's more than just a pet. He can empathize with you—one of the key attributes of a familiar." Her smile broadened.

Perle blinked several times. *A familiar?* It had to be a mistake. Neither of her parents possessed familiars. *What makes me any different?* "That can't be right," she said.

"Familiars will choose their masters, sometimes in the most unlikely ways."

Perle thought about the day her father had given Nuit to her for her tenth birthday. *Did Papa know about Nuit's magical capability?* she wondered. "What does all this mean, Headmistress?"

"It means, because he is your familiar, he may remain here with you. However, you'll be required to take some new classes. I'll see that your schedule is adjusted accordingly."

More classes. Perle frowned slightly and glanced down at her satchel sitting next to her chair. More classes meant less time to investigate the mysterious magic or learn to read more of her rune book. "Very well," she said.

The headmistress stood from her desk and clapped her hands together, her flawless, lightly powdered face brightening. "What an exciting time for you, Ms. Durand, and it's only the beginning of your third week. This is the heart of what Once Upon Academy is about—the discovery of one's true potential."

Perle exhaled. The headmistress had spared her again and seemed to not be aware that Perle was trying to solve the mystery herself. *It's probably best that I keep it a secret for now.* "Merci, Headmistress, for all your generosity," she said.

The headmistress gave her a small wave. "I look forward to hearing great news about your progress. You're dismissed."

Perle stood, grabbing her satchel, then nodded politely to the headmistress. "*Au revoir.*" She spun on her heel and left the office. Even after the door shut behind her, Perle could still feel the headmistress watching her.

CHAPTER 9

Perle raced down the stairs from the headmistress's quarters and joined the sea of students scrambling to and from their classes. She waded through the crowd and headed straight for the library, determined to continue her investigation. A commotion nearby startled her as she reached the library's double doors. A group of students stood in a circle, observing a faculty member within.

"Whose animal is this? Speak up now!" a man barked.

Perle scanned the crowd of onlookers and spotted Ben, who was observing the scene, his brow furrowed pensively. Relieved to see him again, Perle approached him and tapped his shoulder. "Ben, what happened?"

He flinched and looked over his shoulder. Then his face brightened. "Hey! Glad you're here. You might want to… uh…" He gestured toward the center of the circle.

Craning her neck, she peered through the crowd at the faculty member holding up a small black cat by the scruff of its neck. Perle gasped, recognizing the illusion professor. "Master Faust! And he has Nuit!" she hissed to Ben.

Ben nodded solemnly.

"If no one claims this animal, then it will be removed from the premises," Master Conrad Faust announced, holding Nuit up higher for all to see.

Perle shoved her way through the crowd and reached the middle. "That cat is mine, Master Faust."

He looked down his nose at her and narrowed his eyes. "You *do* realize there is a no-pet policy here, do you not, Ms. Durand?" he asked icily.

Perle nodded. "Oui, but Nuit is my familiar, not my pet." She cleared her throat. "The headmistress officially confirmed it."

The older man's dark eyebrows shot up. "Is that so?" He opened his mouth to say more, when the sounds of cheery bird tweets trilled from above.

Perle looked up and noticed Azure perched in the candelabra hanging overhead. The bluebird eyed her briefly then cocked his head.

"Ah..." Master Faust looked up. "I see now." He handed Nuit to Perle then cleared his throat. "Do keep a closer eye on your familiar next time, Ms. Durand."

She took Nuit graciously and cuddled him, relief spreading through her like a wave. She watched Master Faust take his leave then looked back up at the candelabra, but Azure was gone. *Was the headmistress watching all this time?* she wondered, chewing her bottom lip. The circle of spectators dissipated, and the students continued on their way.

Nuit let out a long meow. Perle tilted her head slightly as she stared into the cat's intriguing golden eyes. Calmness washed away the stress in her body. She blinked once and stared at Nuit again.

Purring, he broke the stare then rubbed the side of his face against her.

"I wish I understood what you were trying to tell me," Perle murmured. "How did you get here, anyway? Did Anala let you out?" She would make it a point to speak with her roommate. "Either way, you shouldn't be wandering around here alone. Don't do that again. Not everyone believes you're my familiar yet."

"A familiar, eh?" Ben came up behind her. "Is it true?"

"It's a long story," Perle shook her head. "And now's not the time to talk about that." She started for the library again.

"Where are you going?" Ben called.

She stopped in front of the double doors and placed her hand on the brass handle. She glanced down at her satchel. "It's my responsibility to find out and fix what's been happening around here," she said. She entered the library and made her way upstairs to an empty table in the runic section, where she had initially encountered the fire beetle. She glanced around, making sure none of the faculty were nearby, then reached into her bag and pulled out her rune book.

Nuit hopped up on the table and sat. He stared at the book a moment then let out a low yowl. Somehow, Perle could sense the frustration and fear in his voice. *Is this what the headmistress was talking about when she said that familiars can empathize with their masters?*

"You sense something's amiss?" she whispered to the cat. She glanced around the aisles, anticipating the appearance of another creature, but nothing happened. She held the book in her hands and stared at the embossed rose on the cover. The book gave off a subtle purple glow, then it emanated a soothing warmth. Perle gritted her teeth. *That glow. What's it doing? What's about to happen?* she thought.

"Perle." Ben gently tapped her on her shoulder, severing her thoughts. "I've been meaning to show you this."

She blinked and spun around. Ben held out a thick book entitled *Magical Creatures of Conjuration.*

She raised her eyebrows. *Conjuration?*

"After all the incidents that happened yesterday, I did some research on the nature of the creatures we encountered," Ben explained. "Apparently, there are a lot of different types of creatures that can only be summoned through the art of conjuration. I even found that same spider we encountered in the basement in this book."

"I think it's more than that, Ben." Perle traced her finger along the book cover. "There's something odd about this book. Nuit can sense it too. The more I've thought about it, the more I've realized that these creatures only seem to appear while I have this book present."

A small crease appeared at his brow. "If your book was responsible for those creatures appearing, then this situation may be far worse than we thought," he said. "Deciphering its magic is beyond your or my expertise. We should take it to the headmistress right away."

"Take what to the headmistress?"

Perle jumped at Zeke's gruff voice, which sent a shiver down her spine. She looked up and noticed Zeke leaning against one of the nearby bookshelves, his arms folded across his broad chest. He regarded Perle and Ben with a rigid expression.

She paled and cleared her throat. *How long was he there?* she thought. As she met his pointed stare, her cheeks become scalding hot. "Um…"

Ben grumbled.

Zeke pushed himself off the bookshelf and approached. "What are you two up to?" His gaze bounced from Perle to Ben, and he sneered. "And don't even think about lying to me."

Perle casually leaned her elbow over the book, doing her best to cover it. "I'm trying to get to the bottom of this mystery. I think we're onto something."

Zeke snarled. "What do you think you're onto?"

"The source of the creatures appearing, for one," Perle said. Her hands stung with a sudden painful shock. She grunted, releasing the book, and recoiled. A dim halo of purple light surrounded the book as it hovered in the air before the three of them. A single beam of light shot out from the book and hit something behind her.

"Whoa!" Ben exclaimed.

Zeke stepped in front of Perle, throwing his arm out protectively.

Nuit hissed. Perle looked over her shoulder in time to see the conjuration book in Ben's hands give off a similar eerie purple glow from the hovering book's beam of light. Then Ben's book fell to the ground, and its glowing halo disappeared.

A wall of blue light surrounded the three of them. The bookshelves, the walls, the stairs—the entire library disappeared beyond the surrounding translucent wall and morphed into an endless void of swirling fog.

Perle's heart pounded. *Where are we?* she wondered. *Is this an illusion, or are we truly in another world?*

"Get away from that book, Ben!" Zeke barked over his shoulder, his voice startling Perle from her thoughts.

Ben froze, his arm outstretched as he reached for his conjuration book. He looked toward Zeke then straightened and backed away until he bumped against the translucent wall. "Ugh. What's happening?"

Zeke glared at Perle, his eyes flashing a deep gold. "Disable the spell."

Perle blinked. "What? I don't know how to do that."

"It's your book that's doing it, isn't it?"

"Oui, but—"

A familiar-sounding gibberish chanting filled the room. A bright white light suddenly flashed from Perle's floating book. Electric purple energy shot from it, freezing Ben in place and turning him into a grey stone statue.

Perle gasped. "Ben!"

Zeke's eyes widened, and he got on all fours. He grunted as his body grew bigger and more muscular in a matter of seconds. His clothes ripped to shreds and fell in a tattered heap on the ground. Greyish-white hair covered his body. His shifting complete, he crouched low to the ground and snarled, his body twitching and ready to pounce on the floating book.

Nuit yowled and scrambled between Perle's ankles.

Zeke's deep growling sent a ripple of fear through every nerve in Perle's body. She took several deep breaths, trying to regain her composure. She clenched her fists and attempted to concentrate on one of her two evocation spells. *Ugh. Why is this so hard?*

The floating book flashed again, and Zeke leapt at it, saliva dripping from his open jaws. But just as he was about to collide with the book, he was knocked back by an invisible forcefield. A large spider emerged from the conjuration book under a shroud of purple light. The spider hissed as it crawled toward Zeke, who lay on the ground, disoriented.

"Down, puppy."

Startled, Perle looked for the source of the female voice. A figure emerged from the floating book in a wisp of purple smoke. The figure manifested as a beautiful woman with smooth skin, dark eyes, and short, ebony hair. She stood before them, her long black-and-purple robes flowing in a nonexistent wind. Affixed to her heart was a familiar-looking rose brooch. Her full lips parted, and she smiled sweetly at the three of them. "So nice to see you again, Perle."

Perle did a double take. *That voice. That brooch...* "G-Giselle?"

The woman chuckled. "No, you gullible little fool. My name is *Tilda*."

Tilda… where have I heard that name before? Perle wondered.

The mysterious woman casually flicked her hand toward the spider. The creature launched a blast of webbing around Zeke, confining the wolf in a large white cocoon.

Perle shivered as she watched the spider stand guard over its confined prey. The fear in her veins was replaced with anger. Her friends were at the mercy of dark magic, and she was about to be next. *Oh, no you don't.*

She faced the woman and attempted to calm her nerves in order to focus on her Flaming Hands spell, the only spell she'd felt confident in casting successfully.

"Thank you for bringing me back to Once Upon Academy again," Tilda began. "Now that your job is done, you can enjoy your new home here in the endless voids, where you will no longer be a bother." She laughed darkly.

The woman's voice rattled her mind, and she lost focus. "Why are you doing this? I've done nothing to you!"

Tilda's eyes narrowed, and she turned her nose up at Perle. "Your existence is a constant reminder of Beau's terrible mistake. *I* loved him. He should have chosen *me*. I'll make sure he doesn't make that mistake again. But first, there are some people at Once Upon Academy who I want to exact my revenge on for ruining my life."

Perle's jaw dropped, and she suddenly remembered. "So *you're* the batty woman who wouldn't stay away from him."

"Is that what he told you?" Tilda snarled. "Well, he lied to you, girl. He was completely into me."

"All he did was say 'hi' to you."

Tilda's eyes narrowed. "You have no idea what happened. I was one of the top students at Once Upon Academy. I'd garnered the interest of most of the guys in the school, but they were only interested in my elite student status. Beau, however, was different. He was the only one who cared enough to look beyond my status and actually talk to me. I knew from the first moment that he was the one.

"But he had friends who fed him lies about me, telling him I was an evil witch just because I was interested in researching the darker side of magic. He rejected me every chance he got, even after graduation. I tried one last time to get him to marry me, but with his head full of lies, he said some horrible things to me. So I put a spell on him and turned him into the evil beast of a man that he was.

"For years, I watched him suffer alone and miserable. I wanted him to feel what I felt every time he rejected me. But then Jolie, your mother, came along and ruined everything." Tilda balled her hands into fists. "She'll also be joining you shortly, as will those responsible for locking me away in a magical prison for crimes I didn't commit."

Perle's heart thumped. She was hesitant to believe Tilda's story. Moreover, she couldn't let Tilda get away with her wicked intentions. "Capturing us won't change my parents' love. Papa's love for my mother is forever. He will never love someone as wicked as you!"

Tilda seethed. Her brooch glowed a sinister green. "Enjoy rotting in this abyss, Perle Durand. I shall be going now."

Perle glanced at the brooch and frowned. *That must be the source of her power.* She felt clarity, focus, calm. Something furry rubbed against her calves. The light vibrations of Nuit's purring filled her body with warmth and assurance. She looked down, and the cat stared back at her—or rather through her—his golden eyes giving off a soft, intriguing glow.

The spell was clear in her mind. *Frost Beam.* She glared back at Tilda. "Stop! You're not going anywhere." She moved her hands in a specific pattern, perfect and articulate, as though the spell came naturally to her. She knew exactly what she had to do and how to do it.

"*Glacies trabem!*" she chanted, extending her hands in Tilda's direction.

Her hands tingled then grew numb from an icy chill that ripped from her fingers all the way up her arms. Nuit yowled, his energy amplifying the spell's sensation. A light-blue beam shot from her palms. She directed the beam toward the rose brooch, encasing the flower in ice. Its bright-red petals lost their luster. Small white cracks appeared in the ice's crystalline surface, which shattered. The rose petals withered, detached from the brooch, and fluttered toward the ground. The petals disintegrated before they could land.

The image of Tilda flickered as she gasped and placed her hand to her chest, a shocked look on her pale face.

Perle blinked. *She's an illusion?*

"No!" Tilda shrieked, her image growing ghostly transparent. "You haven't even begun to understand my powers, Perle Durand. This isn't over." She disappeared in a flash of glittering white light.

The glow around Perle's floating book disappeared, and the book fell to the ground with a thump. The giant spider guarding the cocoon containing Zeke looked at her with its many eyes, its chelicerae quivering nervously. Then the creature became transparent and disappeared.

Perle gasped. *Another illusion.* The webbed cocoon disappeared, and Zeke collapsed to the ground in his wolf form. She rushed to his side and touched his soft grey fur, which was slightly damp and tangled from sweat. "Zeke?" she said softly.

The wolf's golden-yellow eyes shot open. In a flash, he was back on his feet, his body crouched low. A deep growl rumbled in his throat as he looked around with sharp, wary eyes.

"It's okay. She's gone," Perle assured him.

Zeke's body shuddered as he observed the endless void around him.

Perle checked on Ben next. He was still stuck in his frozen pose, his arm shielding his fear-stricken face. As she approached him, tiny cracks appeared in his stony body. Suddenly, the statue shattered, and Ben appeared in his normal form. He slumped to the ground amid the tiny shards of rock.

Groaning, Ben held the back of his head and looked up with a disoriented expression. "Ugh. What happened?"

"Long story," Perle said, shaking her head. "We need to find a way to get out of this dreaded place."

Ben nodded and got up. He picked up his conjuration book and looked at it curiously. "What kind of magic could have done this?" He ran his hand over the now-singed cover.

Perle cautiously approached her open rune book lying on the ground. As she drew closer, she noticed the contents of the pages were no longer runes but legible words about roses. The book had become a botany book once again, hopefully for good.

The runes... they're gone... she thought. She was kneeling to pick up the book when Zeke gave a low growl from behind her. Perle looked over her shoulder. By his piercing glare, she assumed he wanted to take the book instead. Now that the mystery was solved, it was probably best that she surrender the book to the headmistress. "Okay. But be careful," she told Zeke, slowly backing away.

Zeke sniffed the book once then seized it in his jaws. As he lifted the book, the hazy void around them suddenly fizzled away, and they were once again in the library. A group of students and faculty surrounded them. Low murmurs swept through the crowd of wide-eyed spectators.

Perle blinked. *Is Tilda's spell broken?* She looked toward the spectators, wondering if they were real. Then Hazel emerged from the crowd and acknowledged the three of them with a stern gaze. She folded her arms over her chest.

"Miss Durand. Mister Wolfson. Mister Spriggan." Hazel addressed them with an icy edge to her voice. "I warned you all before about casting spells in the library. Now you'll answer to the headmistress for your continuous insolence!"

Perle swallowed and looked warily at her friends. Seeing the genuine fear and hesitation in Zeke's golden eyes and the way he curled his tail between his hind legs made her fear the worst.

CHAPTER 10

PERLE ROCKED BACK AND FORTH on the edge of her chair outside the headmistress's office. She wrapped her arms around her midsection as she tried to make sense of all that had happened. She wondered if everything she, Ben, and Zeke had experienced was just a dream.

But it felt too real to be a dream, she thought.

Upon their return to the library from their horrific trip through the void of Tilda's magical illusions, Hazel, the librarian, promptly confiscated the botany book from Zeke and marched them straight to the headmistress's office. Perle knew she would probably never see her book again, but she hoped at least whatever curse had been upon it was gone after Tilda's defeat.

A gentle rumble drew her attention to her calf. Nuit sat with his body leaned up against her, purring lightly. He seemed calm and peaceful despite all that had happened. She smiled at the cat. "That was amazing what you did, the way you helped me control my powers. It felt incredible. Merci, Nuit," she said.

Nuit looked up and meowed in response. Perle felt a gentle calming wave in her mind, as though the cat were trying to reassure her.

"I still don't fully understand all this 'familiar' stuff, but I hope you and I will continue to help each other." She looked from the cat to Zeke, who sprawled in a chair beside her, back in his human form and wearing nothing but a purple-and-black-striped towel wrapped around his waist.

Zeke looked straight ahead, not acknowledging Perle, his eyes dark and brooding.

Ben sat on the other side of her. His elbow rested on the arm of his chair with his cheek nestled against his fist.

This would be the third time in a week that Perle paid a visit to the headmistress. Only serious troublemakers made such frequent visits. Surely the headmistress's generosity had its limits.

Nuit perked up and looked toward the closed double doors of the headmistress's office as the muffled voices beyond increased in volume. Then the doors swung open, and Hazel stepped out. Her blue eyes pinning Perle, Ben, and Zeke, she beckoned them with a wave of her hand. "The headmistress will see you now," she said.

Perle swallowed the nervous lump forming in the back of her throat. She slowly slid out of her chair and followed

Hazel inside the office with Zeke and Ben close behind.

The headmistress sat behind her desk, her hands folded neatly, and watched them, a blank expression adorning her lightly powdered face.

"Thank you, Hazel. That'll be all." The headmistress flicked her hand dismissively at the librarian.

Hazel gave her a polite nod and left.

Perle dared to look into the headmistress's eyes, trying to sense her intention, but her expression was unreadable. Perle wondered what Hazel had told the headmistress. She looked sideways at Zeke, who kept his head lowered. She never thought she would see someone like him so submissive. It was a vulnerable side of him that she respected. She inched her hand to his, touching it gently, then clasped her fingers with his. He tensed, and he swiveled his head to gaze sidelong at her a moment before turning away again.

To her left, she reached out to Ben's dangling hand, clasping it tightly and giving him a reassuring smile. Ben looked back at her then gave her a small, hopeful smile that was short-lived.

"It seems there has been a lot of excitement around here lately," the headmistress began, looking at each of them in turn. Her gaze settled on Zeke. "Care to enlighten me, Mr. Wolfson?"

Zeke opened his mouth then closed it and looked thoughtful. "I... only remember being in a strange dark place," he began. "Then some strange woman appeared, and a spider..." He rubbed his temples as if struggling to remember.

"Interesting." The headmistress flicked her attention to Perle. "And what about you, Ms. Durand?"

Perle took a deep breath. *Will she still believe me?* "Ah..." She cast a glance at Ben and Zeke, then she closed her eyes and recounted the horrific encounter as vividly as if she were reliving it. She felt Nuit's gentle purring against her legs as she spoke, his presence reassuring and calming her. When Perle finished her story, the headmistress leaned back in her chair, her face remaining unchanged as she digested the information.

Ben straightened. "Wait, I was a statue? I don't remember that."

"Of course you don't." Perle shook her head.

A tiny crease appeared at the headmistress's brow. "Your story... doesn't sound possible. The academy is protected with several types of magical wards to prevent such evil influences from entering these grounds."

Evil influences... I wonder how many more times the school has faced trouble, Perle thought. "It's true, Headmistress. The lady we saw had strange power. With Nuit's help, I was able to destroy her rose brooch, which seemed to be the source of her illusion magic."

The headmistress rubbed her chin. "Is that so? Then perhaps..." She looked up and whistled to Azure, who was perched on a small shelf above them. The bluebird flew down and landed on her shoulder. "Allow me to see through Nuit's eyes," she said to Perle.

Perle furrowed her brow, unsure of what the headmistress was requesting. She picked Nuit up and set him on the desk. Nuit took notice of the bluebird. Perle felt his body tense. Azure trilled a lighthearted song, and the cat relaxed.

The headmistress looked at the cat, and her light-brown eyes gave off a soft white glow. Azure continued to sing, and soon the white glow encompassed the bird.

Nuit's golden eyes flashed, as if reacting to the headmistress's strange magic. Then Perle felt another presence, heard a voice, an empathic conversation in her mind. *Show me what you saw. What you felt*, the headmistress urged.

The sensation came as quickly as it went. Perle shook out of her strange trance, as if she were awakening from a long sleep. Nuit meowed and began giving himself a bath.

The headmistress's eyes returned to normal, the glow around her and Azure dissipating. "Extraordinary. What an incredible feat for you both."

Perle sucked in a breath. "Y-you believe me?"

The headmistress's lips stretched into a broad smile. "I saw very vividly how you saved the academy with your brave efforts." She nodded to Zeke and Ben. "All of you."

The two guys perked up.

"That dark magic... I know of it," the headmistress continued. "I've only encountered it once since I became the headmistress." Her smile faded. "I didn't think I would ever encounter it again, but when you mentioned Tilda, I should have known. She was a former student who was obsessed with dark magic. She used her magic recklessly, hurting people. Her obsession with her powers turned her into a dark faerie, too far gone from the ways of good. Eventually, she was found and captured and confined in a magical prison, but it seems she has escaped. It has been so long, I didn't expect her to try to sabotage the school."

"She claimed she loved my father," Perle said. "When he refused her, she put a curse on him that turned him into a beast. I met Tilda in my small town back home. She posed as a kindly bookmobile clerk. I had no idea of her plot to seek revenge on not just my parents but everyone who had hurt her. She tricked me by giving me a cursed botany book."

"Ah, yes, about that book." The headmistress pulled the botany book from behind the desk and set it on the surface.

Perle frowned. Unlike Ben's conjuration book, which had been singed on the cover and nearly destroyed by magic, hers was seemingly untouched, the embossed rose on the cover still as intricate and beautiful as before and gleaming in the light like new. Perle sighed and slumped her shoulders. "It's my fault for bringing it here. I put the entire school in danger because of that book. I'm ready for whatever repercussions are necessary." She noticed, out of the corner of her eye, Ben's head turn slightly to her. His Adam's apple bobbed.

The headmistress gave Perle a questioning look. "Repercussions? If anything, both you and Mister Spriggan were trying to warn everyone of the danger lurking, but it fell on deaf ears. You saved the school and your peers by demonstrating wit, determination, and precise and effective use of the spells you've learned."

Perle exhaled, feeling a great weight lift from her chest. The headmistress's grateful reaction was a pleasant surprise.

"And as for you, Mr. Wolfson." The headmistress turned to Zeke. "It seems now you are beginning to understand your purpose as an RA."

Zeke eyed the woman questioningly. "I'm still not sure that I do, Headmistress."

She let out an airy laugh. "Three semesters ago, you came to me, lost and rejected by your own family. You had no friends. People feared you. And now, because of your bravery, you're hailed and respected as a hero of this school. You've gained a new family and new friends as well." She gave a small head gesture to Perle and Ben.

Perle was happy for Zeke, though a part of her heart still felt troubled for him. She couldn't imagine being rejected by her own family, and she began to understand his rough demeanor. But even as her mother had seen through her father's rough edges, Perle could see a sense of care and compassion in Zeke.

He glanced at Perle and Ben and huffed. "I suppose," he grumbled.

The headmistress clapped her hands together. "This calls for a celebration. Tonight, I'll call for a grand feast in your honor."

Perle beamed. "M-merci, Headmistress!"

"No, Ms. Durand. Thank *you* for believing in yourself." She stood from her chair. "Now, then. You're all dismissed. I'll contact the chefs and event coordinators to see that this feast gets underway this evening… ah, and do grab that fresh pair of clothes sitting by the door on your way out, Mr. Wolfson."

Zeke gave the headmistress a small nod, and headed for the door, securely holding the towel around his waist. He grabbed the small bundle of clothes and took his leave.

Perle picked up Nuit. Her eyes returned to the botany book sitting atop the desk. "Headmistress, if I may ask, what will you do with that book?"

The headmistress's soft expression hardened again, and her lips formed a thin line. "The book will remain with me for the time being, under extensive observation," she said. "I want to ensure there are no more traces of Tilda's dark magic. The more we can learn about the nature of this magic, the better we can protect this school."

"Of course." Perle nodded. *And I hope I never run into Tilda again.* "Au revoir,

Headmistress." She took her leave, and Ben followed.

"A feast, can you believe it? In *our* honor!" Ben strutted alongside Perle and Zeke, who was now fully dressed, down the grand staircase. Nuit followed a few paces behind them.

"I don't need all that recognition," Zeke muttered, his head down as he adjusted a button on one of the cuffs of his black shirt.

"That's exactly what you need," Ben said. "When was the last time anyone recognized you for all the things you have to put up with as an RA?"

Zeke grunted.

Perle walked between her two friends, which she had come to admire and adore. It seemed like yesterday that she'd gone from riding in a fanciful carriage from home to experiencing an adventure she would never forget. It sounded like the beginning of a story, like the many epic books she'd pored over ever since she'd first learned to read.

"So, this means we can all stick together, right?" Ben looked at Perle and Zeke. "Keep an eye on suspicious things around the school and deal with evil magic?"

Zeke snarled. "Don't push your luck, Spriggan."

The three of them reached a set of doors leading to the main atrium, where the buzz of students' voices rose from beyond. Perle stopped at the threshold and turned to her friends. "We couldn't have solved this mystery without working together. Merci to you both." She rose on the balls of her feet and planted gentle kisses on Ben's and Zeke's cheeks. Her face suddenly warmed as she realized what she'd done. *Ah! Did I just kiss them both?*

Zeke and Ben froze, looked at each other, then at Perle, wide-eyed.

Perle smiled, a twinge of confidence leaping into her heart. "See you tonight for the feast." Not sticking around to see or hear their reactions, she rushed out the door.

About the Author

MARIE LONG is an award-winning novelist who enjoys the snowy weather, the mountains, and a cup of hot white chocolate. She's an avid supporter of literacy movements. To learn more about her, visit her website: www.marielongauthor.com.